PASSAGE TO MYTHRIN BOOK 3

THE STARRY

WINDOW

PATRICIA BOW

Cover images:
Starry Sky photo by David W. Siu, used by permission and in accordance with his Creative Commons license.

Sunset at Kynance Cove photo by Danny Chapman, used by permission and in accordance with his Creative Commons license.

Flying Dragon image used by permission of artist and copyright holder Lindsey Goodbun (http://fantasyfauna.yolasite.com/).

This book is for

Vivi and Nora

my two young dragons

What's happened so far

IN *THE RUBY KINGDOM* (Passage to Mythrin Book 1), Amelia Hammer's globe-trotting parents have dumped her in tiny Dunstone to stay with her grandmother, Celeste, and her geeky cousin Simon. Stranded in a small northern town in the middle of winter, Amelia expects to die of boredom before spring.

Simon isn't happy either, saddled with this once-fun cousin who's mutated into a neon-haired stranger. Especially as he's expected to be *nice* to her.

But right away, life in safe little Dunstone turns dangerously exciting. A strange girl appears on their apartment roof in a blizzard wearing nothing at all. Proud, fearless, and totally ignorant of ordinary things like water faucets and oranges, Mara could have dropped from another planet.

Which she did. Mara is the new young chief of the Urdar, the race of shape-changers who rule Mythrin. An ancient system of hidden gates and passages links Mythrin to other worlds. At war with her upstart brother, Mara retreats to Earth through the Dunstone gate to escape an assassin. But the assassin follows, meaning to finish her off, and just too bad for anyone else who gets in his way.

Amelia, Simon, and their friend Ike thwart the assassin and help Mara return to Mythrin, where the war comes to a crisis. The vengeful assassin lures Amelia into a trap, whisking her spirit out of her human body, which remains in Dunstone.

On Mythrin she takes the dominant form of the Urdar. She's suddenly a dragon — powerful, winged, magical — and she's strongly tempted to stay that way. But Simon finds out that if she doesn't come home to Earth, her human form will die.

Amelia must choose. Is she human? Or dragon?

1

IN *THE PRISM BLADE* (Passage to Mythrin Book 2), six months later, Simon and his friend Ike are training for the annual Dunstone and Area Weird Games (DAWG). It's the only athletic competition that favours geeks over jocks, so the boys figure they stand a chance.

Then Mara makes contact, needing Amelia's help. The Casseri, human refugees from another world and age-old enemies of dragons, have come to Mythrin to find the legendary Prism Blade. The Urdar and the Casseri both want the Blade for their own protection. Both fear they'll be slaughtered if the other side gets it first.

The three kids are caught by surprise when they learn that the Prism Blade has been hidden in plain sight in their own town. To get close enough to grab it, they must win the Weird Games. The cousins take opposite sides. Simon wants to help the refugees and their Seeker, Pier. Amelia favours the Urdar. She's made friends with Ty, a young dragon who takes human form (punk-style leather, chains, green hair) when he arrives in Dunstone. What's more, she's developing some dragon powers of her own, sparked by her friendship with Mara.

But soon they all must work together to save the Prism Blade, and their own skins, from Zeph, Mara's ruthless rival. And they need to learn the true nature of the Blade, and wield it themselves, to save both the dragons and the refugees.

Before Simon leaves Mythrin for the last time, Pier shows him a world gate bearing the image of a boy who looks amazingly like himself, reaching up to pluck a star. Which is impossible — it has to be thousands of years old. He feels relieved when he learns that the dragons plan to bury the gates, to protect their world.

Maybe, if he's lucky, he'll never have to solve the riddle of the starry window. Maybe he'll never see Mythrin again.

Chapter 1

A Light Like Thunder

ALL THAT THIRD Friday in October, Amelia felt the storm coming. It ached in her bones, it crawled all over her skin like invisible ants. Distant lightnings sizzled along her nerve endings.

Oddly enough, the day was brightly sunny and the weather channel predicted clear weather for the next week. But Amelia's bones knew better.

It must be a new talent, she thought, something that came with the feeling of scales under the skin and wings folded behind the shoulder blades. Bundled in like extra software. She wouldn't mind getting a few new talents. Being able to take notes in class without actually listening to the teacher: now, that would be useful.

She caught Mr. DeSouza's eye, smiled vaguely, and bent over her notebook again.

But predict the weather? Like I *want* to feel like this?

She'd been jittery all day, and it had to be a storm on the way. Leaves kept ripping off the trees and splatting on the windows, making her flinch. A gust of wind rattled the windows in their cracked frames and she nearly jumped out of her chair.

St. Olav Collegiate Institute was an old school that stood among big, gangly silver maples and chestnuts in Toronto's east end. Locals called this neighbourhood the Beach. Or the Beaches. Amelia had never figured out which was right. Anyway, she'd seen the so-called beaches and they were a joke compared to the ones in British

3

Columbia.

Everything here is so small and old and crowded and grungy. I hate this place. I miss the ocean. I miss Vancouver.

Crazily enough, she also missed little old Dunstone, but mainly that meant her cousin Simon and their grandmother, Celeste. Maybe even Simon's pal Ike, a little. It would've been good to have Simon here to growl at on a day like this.

Leaves flapped on the glass again with a sound like beating wings. *Ty*, she thought. That last thing he'd said, just before she left Mythrin, in June: *It may not be forever.* (Yeah, right.) *Look for me some fine morning.* (Well, that won't be today. If ever.)

But how could she blame him? Ty was flying far and wide over Mythrin, exploring, discovering new gates. Probably helping to block them, too. He was busy with the great work Mara had set going, protecting Mythrin from invaders. He had a lot more important things to do than cross the emptiness between worlds to visit some human kid he hardly knew.

But he told me his full name! He said it — Tynenannarrithen! That had to mean something spe—

"Amelia!"

She looked up into a waiting silence. She knew that silence. It meant a room full of smirks, everybody watching for her to make a fool of herself. She looked Mr. DeSouza straight in the eyes. "Yes?"

"Monster," said Mr. DeSouza.

Amelia's heart flipped. "Uh." She cleared her clogged throat.

"The word 'monster.' It comes up a lot in the *Beowulf* excerpt you read last night."

"Oh!" She almost laughed. *Thought he meant me!*

"You did read it, yes?"

"Sure!" When *was that assigned?*

"Good. What do you suppose it means? The word 'monster.'"

4

What does it usually mean? "Oh — huge, I guess. And horrible."

"But something more in this story, surely?" Mr. DeSouza had a friendly face, but how real was that? "Huge and horrible, yes. But what else?"

Were we supposed to know this? "Well, sort of, you know...."

He tilted his head to one side and waited. Not really a friendly face, no. *Why are you picking on me?*

"Alone," someone whispered behind her, so soft she nearly didn't catch it.

"Uh, it means he's alone?"

"Very good." He looked surprised. "That's right, Grendel is alone. That's what really makes him a monster: not his size, not the way he's like a human, but twisted. The poet says Grendel is cut off from humankind, he dwells in darkness. He walks alone."

Walks alone. Amelia listened to wings beating on the glass. Words washed over her and flowed away.

Language Arts was the last class of the day. She spent as much time as possible rearranging the stuff in her backpack, while listening to the scuff of feet and the scrape of chairs. When she stood up and turned around, there was nobody right behind her. All she saw was a stream of backs heading out the door. She followed them at a safe distance.

Knots of kids stood around outside the front entrance. Amelia passed them without a glance. Chin up, shoulders back, stride long and confident. Like Mara. *Just try and stop me, puny humans!*

She kept it up all the way down the block to Queen Street. Rounded the corner and went back to her usual slouching stroll, hands in pockets.

The air smelled like stale cigarette butts. You could've scooped the smog with a spoon. At the west end of the street — quick glance over shoulder — the sinking sun blazed out of a clear peach-coloured

5

sky. That surprised her. She'd expected to see purple storm clouds boiling up. That about-to-explode feeling was stronger than ever.

Yes! Thunder and lightning, bring it on! That would clear the air.

"Amelia! Wait up!" Shoes thudded on pavement. Petra Nowak fell into step beside her. "What's the big rush?"

Amelia shrugged.

"So watcha think of Mr. DeSouza?" Petra asked.

"Doesn't like me."

"He doesn't like people who blow off the assignments. That was me behind you, btw."

"Oh." Amelia shot a glance at Petra's sharp profile. "Thanks."

"So what are you going to do for the essay?"

"What essay?"

"The one he assigned at the end of class."

Shoot.

They crossed Beryl Street. Amelia stopped in front of an accessories shop she liked, and made herself turn and look up. Petra smiled down at her. The smile was bright, like her pale blond hair, which she wore pulled back into a long ponytail. And it was sharp, like her nose. And it was totally plastic, like her very cool chunky amber bracelet.

Amelia smiled back with all her teeth. "I guess I forgot to write it down."

"You can copy my notes. You want?"

Petra was tall and just thin enough, and at first glance could have been sixteen instead of thirteen. Amelia wished *she* could make a pair of jeans and a black velvet jacket look that good. She herself would probably grow up looking more like her small, slight mother than her tall, muscular father. She knew that, but she didn't have to like it.

"No thanks." She set off along the street again, eyes front. "Why d'you bother?"

"Why would you say that?"

"You're the queen of cool. Got your own fan club."

"Funny." Petra didn't miss a step. "I call them my friends."

"Why you walking this way? You live on my street?"

"No, next block over."

They reached the corner of Queen Street and Chrysoprase Road. Petra came to a halt in front of Pisa Pizza. She grabbed Amelia's arm. "Look, you're new. I'm just trying to help you make friends."

Amelia yanked her arm free. "I can make my own friends, thanks so much."

"You?" Petra laughed. "Little Miss Snot-nose?"

"What did y—"

"That's your name at school, didn't you know that? Swanning around like you bought the place, like you're too good to talk to any—"

"Me? It's everybody else—"

"You're acting like an idiot!"

"Shut up!"

"You've got no friends and it's all your own fault!" Petra yelled.

"Well that's just great, because if I had friends like you I'd jump in front of a bus!"

Petra tossed her hands in the air. "Oh, forget it!" She pushed past Amelia and strode away eastward on Queen Street.

Something made Amelia look sideways. The Pisa Pizza window was full of faces, four or five, all staring at her. Some she knew from school. They must have been watching the fight. Great show, four stars.

She stared back long enough to show she didn't care, then shrugged, turned away and strolled on around the corner. Chrysoprase Road climbed steeply northward, first the shops, then the houses, roof above roof, tree above tree. The roofs and treetops shone golden on one side, where they caught the sun.

Funny how she knew faces but hardly any names. In her old school in Vancouver she'd known everybody. Even in Dunstone she'd had a lot of — well, okay, not friends exactly, but people she could hang with.

Little Miss Snot-nose.

Amelia jammed her fists in her pockets. Fists helped.

It was all turned inside out. From the very first day it was *them* being snotty, especially the girls, always whispering and giggling in their little cliquey knots. Watching her like she was some kind of freak.

So Amelia had put on her bravest face, the way Mara had taught her. Darned if she was going to go begging to be let inside somebody's magic circle. And *damned* if she'd be lumped in with the outsiders: the dummies, the nerds, the brainiacs.

I'll make my own clique, just me. I walk alone. Yeah, like Grendel.

The house she lived in now stood on the crest of the hill. It was one of those big old houses about a hundred years old that had odd corners and turrets and chimneys all over.

When they moved to Toronto in August, Amelia had begged her parents to rent a nice new apartment on the thirtieth floor of one of those shiny buildings downtown, but her dad said no, those cost a mint.

Her mother said they were planning to buy a home in the Beach (Beaches?) someday, so they might as well rent there while they looked around for just the right place. The two-storey-plus-loft apartment in Mrs. Pearson's house was spacious and clean, the house was just a few blocks from Amelia's new school, and Mrs. Pearson lived on the ground floor and had agreed to clean once a week and provide the occasional frozen casserole, which was good, because

8

Amelia's parents were too busy to cook half the time.

"And you can go to her flat if ever we're really late getting home. It's perfect!"

Her parents must have noticed Amelia wasn't bubbling with joy, because they gave her the fourth-floor loft, which used to be the attic, for her bedroom. She was still mad at them for dragging her all over Canada and dumping her here and there without any say, so she wouldn't give them the satisfaction of admitting she actually . . . sort of . . . well, liked the house. Bits of it, anyway. Her roof eyrie, for one thing.

At the top of the hill, Amelia turned in at the paved lane that ran between the south side of the house and a row of yellow Lombardy poplars. Round the back, instead of a yard or garden there was a small parking lot, and the Hammer family's private entrance, a wooden staircase that led up to the second floor.

Amelia looked up at the house, a black hulk against the bright peach-coloured sky. It was — she glanced at her watch — it was just past four. Her parents wouldn't be home until six or later. She didn't want to be alone up there in the creaky silence while the sun set and the twilight crept in. "All old houses make noises," her father had told her, but to Amelia those tiny creaks always sounded like someone sneaking up behind her.

Well, I can't hang around out here. Shape up, Amelia!

She set her foot on the stairs.

That was when things went strange.

The golden light died. The air took on a sullen greenish tint, the light you get before a really bad thunderstorm.

Amelia felt queasy. *I'm sick. I'm going to pass out.* The thought brought relief. *That's what this is all about. Sick.* But she didn't pass out.

The door at the top of the stairs had a small window in it. A face

9

looked out through the glass. Amelia ran up the stairs. "Mom! Dad!"

She stopped two steps below the landing. It wasn't mom or dad up there. The face was strange, long and pale and yet shadowed, as though it was staring out through murky green water.

And then it wasn't strange. It was....

"Ty! You came back!" Amelia leaped up the steps. She pounded her hands on the door. "Ty!" she laughed.

He didn't smile. Didn't even seem to see her. He looked right past her and his face was stiff with horror and fear and disbelief.

Then he turned away and faded into greenish darkness.

Amelia dumped her backpack, scrabbled out her keys, nearly dropped them down the stairs, got the door unlocked and crashed inside. She stood panting, trying to listen. The flat was silent except for those sinister creaks.

"Ty? Where are you?"

The strange greenish light was gone. The room was full of swaying shadows, a tree-scattered sunset. That wasn't much better.

"Ty!"

No answer. Amelia ran from room to room, upstairs and down, calling and calling. No Ty, nowhere. Nowhere.

Chapter 2

Kevin and the Quints

AT FIVE O'CLOCK on the third Friday in October, Simon was sitting at a small, round iron table on the street outside Dunn River Books, translating *The Promise of Quantum Computing*, by H. J. Fehmerheim, into French.

This was one of his favourite places to go after school. He could watch traffic and people, drink coffee, do his homework. Maybe, if he was lucky, spot Dinisha Rajeev, who liked to come downtown with her friends.

Today's homework was turning out to be harder than he'd expected. It was actually not just today's, but this semester's special French class project. Translate five pages of any book that wasn't already published in French, that was the assignment. The translations would be printed together in a booklet, with copies for the whole class.

Simon chose *The Promise of Quantum Computing* because — well, admit it — he wanted to impress Dinisha. She was without a doubt the smartest niner at Dunstone Secondary. Simon had been a little in love with her ever since Grade two, when she'd sat down beside him in the games corner and put together all the puzzles inside fifteen minutes.

Besides, he thought a book on quantum would be easy, because of all the math in it. Not so many words to translate.

But after twenty minutes, he was only halfway through the first paragraph. An awful lot of these words weren't in the English-French dictionary. He had a feeling they might not even be in the regular English dictionary.

Simon sighed, flipped the book closed, and reached into his jeans pocket for the Mythrin stone.

Lying on his palm, just a chunk of smooth, grey stone, it looked completely ordinary. But it wasn't: it was the rarest piece of rock on Earth. It came from Mythrin, another world in another universe. Because it came from there, you could use it to open a gate to that world.

Even more special was the star-shaped splash of dried dragon's blood on one side. There wasn't another piece of rock on Earth marked that way. Simon was pretty sure drops of dragon's blood were very, very scarce, on this or any other planet.

He always kept the Mythrin stone in his pocket, along with his key collection and the hand-polished chestnut from last fall, and his overstuffed leather wallet. It was a lucky stone, if ever there was one. Something to touch when he needed courage. Gripped in his fist, it reminded him of the times he'd surprised himself: when he'd taken risks, when he'd jumped into the unknown.

He'd even faced up to a dragon, once or twice. Compared to that, how scary could it be to — for example — ask Dinisha to work with him on a science project?

It was also proof that Mythrin did exist, and he and Amelia and Ike had really gone there. He needed that reminder. As the months passed, the memory of Mythrin had started to fade like a dream.

He hadn't much hope of ever using the stone to get to Mythrin again. Just as well. That meant he would never have to worry about the starry window, that world gate on Mythrin with his image on it.

Can't get there. No need to worry. Don't need to think about it.

But he still couldn't help thinking about it.

12

"HEY! Hey, Simon!"

Oh, no. He hadn't even seen them coming. He stuck the Mythrin stone in his pocket. "Oh, hi, Kevin." Only it wasn't just Kevin. The table was surrounded.

Kevin Purcell by himself was bad enough. He used to be okay, just kind of loud. But lately, he never lost a chance to heckle Simon or Ike. Ike said Kevin blamed them for making him lose the Weird Games last summer, "like the competition belonged to him, the butthead."

But Kevin with his five buddies was five times worse.

The buddies weren't related. They all had different last names. Their first names were Terry, Shawn, Ryan, Max and Casey, but Simon could never remember which was which. They always stuck together ("like Siamese quintuplets," Ike said). When Kevin sneered the others snarled, and when Kevin joked they fell down laughing.

They were grinning now. It was written all over their faces: *This is gonna be fun!*

"Hey Si! Watcha reading?" Kevin scooped the book off the table. Simon tried to grab it, but Kevin waved it high in the air. "Quantum computing! Oh, man!"

Simon pushed back his chair and stood up. "Give it back, Kevin."

"But isn't this stuff too *hard* for you?"

"Give it back!" Simon reached for the book. Kevin tossed it over his head. One of his buddies caught it and tossed it back. "Hey!" Simon swiped for it, and missed. "Careful! It's a library book!"

"A library book!" Kevin giggled. "Careful! Don't drop it!" He flung it high in the air.

Next thing Simon knew, Kevin and the quintuplets were running around and around the table, screaming with laughter and tossing the book back and forth.

Simon leaped after the flapping thing, knowing how useless that was, but no better plan came to mind. Except to punch Kevin, and he knew how that would end. With himself splattered all over the sidewalk.

All the same he was bracing himself to do just that, when a voice thundered "Cease!" and Kevin stopped dead.

It flashed into Simon's head that the enormous voice had cast a spell on the world. For one moment everything seemed to stop. Not just Kevin. The cars, the wind in the trees, the fluttering awnings. All sound, too. Dead still.

Then he shook his head, and his ears cleared, and the world crashed to a start. Two of the quints barrelled into Kevin like traffic piling up on the 401. The other three tripped over the first two and each other, and sprawled.

The book dropped to the ground. Simon scooped it up. Then he looked at Kevin.

Kevin wasn't moving. He struggled. Two huge hands held him down, one on each shoulder. A shape as big as the voice towered behind him. "Villains!" boomed the man. "Flap-eared knaves! Book destroyers! In what pigsty were you born? Get you gone, you unmannered dogs!"

He shook Kevin back and forth like a handful of wilted dandelions, then let him go. Kevin windmilled forward, caught his balance, and spun around. His friends scrambled to get behind him. "You — crazy — jerk!" Kevin croaked. "You're dangerous! I'm gonna report you to the cops!"

The man waved them away like flies. They ran across the street towards the mall and stopped on the opposite sidewalk. "Hey Simon!" Kevin yelled. "You be careful! You hang with morons and crazies, you could end up in the loony bin!" The six of them swaggered off, hooting and punching each other.

The man wasn't looking at them. "Boy," he said in a voice like very distant thunder, "show me the book."

"It's just a bit torn."

"Then I will mend it." He held out a hand the size of a dinner plate, palm up. Simon placed the book on it. The man carried it inside the bookstore. Simon fished his backpack out from under the table and followed.

Now that he'd had time to think, he realized who this must be. It was John Lilac, Dunstone's mystery man. He'd turned up out of nowhere last July: nameless, homeless, speechless, memoryless. But harmless too, or so he seemed. The owner of Dunn River Books, Vesper Wynn, had given him a job and a place to stay.

He hardly ever showed his face outside the bookstore. He was strange, even the dogs knew it: they barked at him on the street. Kids at school said he was cracked.

He had plenty of language now, but it was all strange. He'd picked it up from the books, people said. Not surprising the way he talked, the books Vesper would give him to read. Shakespeare and Milton and that sort of thing.

The bookstore took up the first floor of a tall old house that backed on a lane next to the gorge. It shouldn't have been dark inside — there were lights and windows — but it was so crammed, floor to ceiling, with bookshelves, and each shelf was stuffed so full, that it seemed dark to Simon.

Maybe the books soaked up the light, he thought. Especially since they were used books, not as fresh and shiny as new ones. The place smelled of old paper and dust. A cave of books, with the mystery man holed up in it.

John Lilac carried *The Promise of Quantum Computing* behind the cash desk, which stood near the shop's front window. "This tape," he said, picking up a roll in his long, thin fingers, "is excellent physic for books."

Simon stared at the hands as they worked. Why did they look so weirdly long? Then he saw. They looked long because they were long. The middle three fingers had four joints instead of the usual three. The nails were narrow, with a faint blue tinge at the inner end.

In a minute the rip was mended. John Lilac closed the book and held it soothingly between his palms, then handed it back.

"Thanks," Simon said. "For, um, everything."

John Lilac looked at him. Simon looked back. There really was something strange about him. Not just the hands. What was it? A tall man with a big, rangy frame, all bone and muscle. Jeans and a dark blue cotton shirt, nothing odd there. Thick black hair that fell over his forehead, a long dark face, and eyes . . . .

That was it, the eyes. They were the clear blue-purple of lilacs, which is why Vesper had given him that name, since he couldn't remember his real one. They shone with a startling brightness in his dark face.

They were shining at Simon now. What with scattering Kevin's gang and fixing the book, Simon guessed, Lilac hadn't paid any attention to him until this minute. It seemed to be his way to give all his attention to one thing at a time. And now that one thing was Simon's face.

"I feel I must know you," John Lilac rumbled softly.

"Well, I, uh, I don't think . . ." Simon didn't like the way the man was staring at him. Eyes like lasers!

"I have seen you before this, surely. And there is an air, a scent of … Who are you? What do you carry?"

"I, uh, I …." Simon backed towards the door.

John Lilac stepped out from behind the desk. "What is that in your pocket, boy? Answer!" Suddenly he seemed twice as big, twice as dark. His eyes glittered like amethysts.

16

Simon could hardly breathe. This was nuts. Maybe Kevin was right: maybe Lilac was dangerous. He turned and shoved out of the door to the safety of the street.

Just then people started shouting over by the mall. Something was happening. There was a guy running — running this way, a guy with a wild mop of hair. Blue-green hair! Stranger yet, he was wearing nothing. Not a thing. Not even underwear.

Simon stared in wonder. He had never been able to figure out why a person would want to take off all their clothes and run around naked in public. To get attention, maybe? If so, this guy, young, could be a teenager, was getting plenty of attention.

Whooping with laughter, he raced across the street past braking, screeching, honking cars and pickups. A couple of security guards from the mall and two OPP constables came thudding after him in their heavy boots, and a comet's tail of yelling kids led by Kevin streamed behind them.

The laughing streaker with the blue-green hair was sprinting straight for the Dunn River gorge. East of the bookstore, the houses ended and only a walking trail and a chest-high stone wall separated the ninety-foot drop from King Street. At the wall he slid to a stop, looked back over his shoulder, and...

"Hey!" Simon shouted. The guy couldn't know what he was doing. "No! Not that way!"

The streaker flashed a grin in Simon's direction. Then he slapped a hand on the parapet, leaped, and was gone.

Chapter 3

Men of Mystery

AFTER TWO WEEKS of rainstorms, the river was running high and furious. The torrent crashed on the rocks far below. Flecks of foam chilled Simon's face as he leaned over the parapet.

Anybody who fell into that would be battered to bits. Maybe killed.

"You'd think we'd see him, though," he said to the nearest of the two hulking mall guards standing next to him at the parapet. "Unless he sank." The guard didn't answer.

"Hey, Simon!" A big paw slapped him on the back. Oscar Vogelsang, Ike's dad and the editor of the *Dunstone Independent*, hulked on his other side. Hulked even more than the mall guards, in fact, because he was fat as well as big. "What's going on?"

Oscar already had his camera out. He always turned up when anything happened, as if he could smell it in the wind. ("He calls it his newsman's nose," Ike said.)

"A guy jumped," Simon began, but the nearer guard cut him off.

"Some creep," he growled over Simon's head. "Musta been stoned or crazy, maybe both. We found him wandering around the mall, mother-naked. Then he ran out here and jumped."

"When'd you first see him? Around five?" Oscar was scribbling at top speed in a little notebook, which he had braced on Simon's shoulder. "How'd he get in the mall like that? Did he walk in *au naturel* or take his clothes off there?"

"Who knows?" the other guard snarled. "Anyway, he's dead now. No loss."

Oscar's pen paused. "I see he marked you up pretty good, Number Two. Nice shiner. Who started the rumpus?"

"Don't answer that," said the first guard to the second. Simon looked up at them, but from here they looked the same, like two slabs of concrete wearing identical burgundy blazers and grey flannel pants, with identical bald buzz cuts and mirror sunglasses. Their name badges said Dunstone Heritage Lanes Security One and Dunstone Heritage Lanes Security Two.

"Somebody's got to know something," Oscar said. "Who was he? Where did he come from?"

"Don't know and don't care," said Security One. "Leave it to the cops."

The two OPP constables, Lisa Nader and Bob Lebrun, had climbed down into the gorge to search along the waterline, one on each side.

"Um," said Simon. "Where are his clothes? Maybe they'll have some clues about who he is. Maybe a wallet."

"Of course!" Oscar beamed at him. "Kid, you're a genius!" He lumbered, surprisingly fast, towards the mall. The mall guards ran after him, shouting. Kevin and the quints ran after them.

The half-dozen people who had gathered walked away, shaking their heads. John Lilac was not among them. He didn't seem to like crowds.

The sun was down, the sky was darkening. The river's roar sounded angry and sad, like a caged lion. Simon started home.

THE HAMMER FAMILY had always owned the building at the corner of King Street and Wallace, two blocks west of the bookstore. You could read the words THE HAMMER BLOCK 1922 carved

19

over the front door. At three storeys high it was one of the tallest buildings in town.

Simon and Celeste lived there in an apartment on the second floor, but the apartment would be dark and deserted now. It was Friday, so his grandmother would be busy until nine o'clock in Boomer Heaven, her authentic 1960s clothing store on the ground floor.

Simon stood outside the store window, looking in. People were fingering the bell-bottom jeans and beaded headbands, and sniffing packages of incense sticks. Celeste, wearing her orange Indian caftan with the gold embroidery, and her little round John Lennon glasses, was holding up a fringed suede vest for a customer and dancing with it to make the fringe sway.

Simon didn't want to be all by himself in the silent apartment, where there would be nothing to stop him thinking about that guy who'd jumped over the parapet. And the way he'd grinned, with a kind of wild glee, before he made that easy leap.

He pushed through the door into Boomer Heaven's sandalwood-scented warmth. Celeste was setting up a display of mood rings, sliding them from her fingers onto the branches of a wooden stand. "Hey, kiddo. Had a good day?" she asked, as soon as she saw him.

"It was okay. Well, maybe not so much. I saw a guy jump in the gorge."

"You what?" Celeste stopped with her fingers spread and stared at him. He told her all about it. She kept shaking her head. "Oh, no. Poor kid," she murmured. "Do they know who he was?"

"Not yet."

"And you. Are you all right?" She turned his head with one finger so she could see his face. Simon realized she had to look up at him now, just a little.

"I think so."

20

She gave him a quick hug and then went back to sliding mood rings from her fingers onto the wooden stand. Watching, Simon suddenly pictured John Lilac's fingers holding a roll of tape.

"What does it mean when a person has blue fingernails?"

"Bad style sense, in my opinion." Celeste gave him a twinkly look. "What girl is this?"

He felt his face heat up. "It's not a girl! It's a man. John Lilac. His nails are sort of blue."

"Then it could mean illness. Which I suppose would not be surprising."

The customer who was looking at the suede vest decided to buy it. That kept Celeste busy for the next five minutes. Simon finished arranging the mood rings on their stand. He didn't know why people spent good money on those things. He'd once worn one a whole day and it hadn't changed colour. "You're not moody enough," Ike had told him.

"Okay," Celeste said, filing the sales slip in its drawer. She took off her Lennon glasses, which were just for show, and gave Simon one of her piercing looks. "What's this about? Did that man give you any trouble?"

"Trouble? No! I just noticed. He's got strange hands."

"The thing about John Lilac," she said, "is that he's an unknown quantity. He could be perfectly safe. We just don't know. He seems to have no idea how to behave around people, although he's getting better, Vesper says. No more repeats of what happened in Stratford."

"Why, what happened?"

Celeste spotted a customer wanting to try on some jeans, so Simon had to wait fifteen minutes for his answer. While waiting he arranged the display of incense sticks on the counter by colour, according to their order in the spectrum, from red through to violet.

"What happened in Stratford?" he asked, when Celeste came

21

back.

"Stratford?" She looked blank a moment. "Oh! Right. Vesper and Lysander — Mr. Manning — took John to see a play at the festival. *Macbeth*, I think it was. He just didn't get it — he thought there was a real murder. Jumped onto the stage to fight the actors. It took four men to drag him out of there."

"Wow!"

"I think Vesper's taking a chance, letting him share a house with her. I suppose she thinks he's harmless because she was the one to find him, and he supposedly trusts her. But then she's always taken chances. Like when she married her second husband. That one ran off with her bank account."

"What happened to the first husband?"

"Ran off with her best friend."

"But she's not going to marry John Lilac, is she?"

"I hope to heaven not! In any case I'm not sure she can, until he gets his memory back. Who knows how many wives he's got stashed away?"

"Or he could be a murderer. Or a spy." He pictured those hands again, and decided not to mention the extra joints. "Or an alien."

Celeste laughed. "Somehow, I don't think so. All the same, be careful around that man."

Simon was thinking about this as he left the shop and climbed the stairs to the apartment. When he opened the door, the phone was ringing. *Dinisha?* He dropped his backpack and crashed into the kitchen. The phone stopped ringing as he snatched it up.

He checked for messages. There were four, all for him. None were from Dinisha — and now that he thought about it, he realized what a stupid hope that was.

They were all from Amelia, all different versions of "Call! Now!" Simon erased the messages, then went to the fridge for a glass of chocolate milk. He had enough to think about. Ammy could wait.

What is that in your pocket? What a weird thing to say! Why would John Lilac care what he had in his pockets? Besides, the only special thing he had was the Mythrin stone. And John Lilac couldn't have known about that, could he?

Simon took it out and looked at it again. He still remembered Pier's face, all pale and solemn, when she'd handed it to him. "That's dragon's blood," she'd said. "Very powerful." He wondered if Pier and her people had moved on yet to a world of their own, a world without dragons.

After coming back from Mythrin at the end of June, he and Ike and Ammy had spent days searching the Internet for anything about dragon's blood. They'd even shivered through an afternoon in the over-cooled new library out on Hill Street, leafing through heavy books.

It was Ammy who found out that the word "dragon" came from an old Greek word that meant "to see clearly."

Besides that there wasn't much, just a few old stories. The best was about a hero named Sigurd, who swallowed a drop of dragon's blood, and after that he understood the language of birds, and the birds told him about a plot to kill him.

"Language of birds!" Ike whooped. "Cool!"

They'd wasted a lot of time creeping up on flocks of sparrows, chickadees, mourning doves, starlings, chickens, finches, pigeons, and gulls, with the stone in hand. Never a word out of them. They also tried out the stone on dozens of dogs, cats and gerbils, a gecko, a bumble bee, several house flies, and a Mennonite carriage horse. Not a word.

THE PHONE RANG again. "Oh, hi, Ammy."

"Finally! I've been calling and calling! Where've you been?"

23

"Out."

"Okay, listen. I'm coming down for the weekend. I'll take the bus to Kitchener tomorrow morning and catch the Dunstone bus from there."

"But I was just with Celeste, down in the shop. She didn't say—"

"I haven't called her yet. Just going to. She's in the shop? Okay, I'll call there. I cleared it with Mom and Dad. I told them I really miss you guys."

"Well, that's nice, but... "

"But that's not the reason. I mean, it's true, but the real reason is I'm going to Mythrin. I need to use that gate. You've still got the stone, right?"

"Sure. But what about Mr. Manning's shed, and the fence —"

"— and the dog, right. Simon, I need you. You and Ike. I need you to think a way around all that so we can get at the gate. You two are good at that stuff."

"But —"

"And this is why."

Simon slid down the wall as he listened, until he was sitting on the floor. "Ty?" he echoed.

"Yeah. Simon, when I saw him in the window — I never ever saw him look like that before. I never knew he *could* look like that. Oh Simon..." Her voice went foggy. "Something awful's happened to him. I *have* to go to Mythrin!"

"But you don't even know where he is!"

"No, but Mara might know. So Mythrin's the place to start. See you tomorrow." She hung up.

Chapter 4

Dreams

SIMON DREAMED he was struggling to climb the steep side of a mountain made of glass. Every time he nearly reached the top, he slid down again and had to struggle back up.

And then a hand reached down from above. "Grab on!" someone called. Simon reached, but before he could grasp the hand, it sprouted claws like a dragon's and snatched at him. He fell in a shower of broken glass.

SIMON WOKE to find himself lying on the floor beside his bed in a tangle of blankets. He lay for a moment, bewildered, then crawled back into bed, dragging the blankets after him.

He slid his hand under the pillow and closed it around the Mythrin stone. It didn't help much, this time. He still felt as if he was falling, as if things were out of his control.

No mystery about what had brought this on. It was Ammy's phone call and her talk of going to Mythrin. Come right down to it, he was scared stiff.

Ike, of course, had been all for going back, last June, as soon as he heard there was a stained glass window showing Simon's image in the Hall of Gates.

"Not yet," Simon said then. He'd wanted time to think about the why and the how of that window. And the who. The only people who could have made that window had been dead and gone for tens of thousands of years. How could they have known he would even exist some day? Let alone be wearing a Dunstone and Area Weird Games T-shirt, and shoes with stars on the ankles?

It made him feel a little better that whoever'd made that window had been dead wrong about the shoes. He didn't own any shoes like that and never would.

He did own a DAWG T-shirt, but that didn't mean anything. Everybody who'd competed in the Weird Games had one. He'd stuffed his into the back of the drawer where he kept the rainbow-striped "Child Power" jersey Celeste had given him on his twelfth birthday, and other unwearable things.

No, that window's impossible. Doesn't mean a thing. Go to sleep.

THE STREAKER woke up. For a moment he thought he knew who he was. A name echoed in his mind, then faded and was gone. He looked at his hands. They looked as if they belonged to someone else. They were too pale, the fingers too stubby, the nails black and broken.

It was still night. A bitter wind whistled past his ears. He shivered with cold and dread, and suddenly knew that wasn't right. Not right for him.

He tried to remember. At first there had been enemies to fight, and battle-heat, and the excitement of the chase. That was all gone now.

And before the battle? He groped back through memory and came up against a blank wall.

What is this place? How did I come here? He lay curled up in a corner where two low walls met: a fence made of squared reddish stones. He had climbed and climbed and found this tower-top covered with pebbles. Here, at least, the painful lights did not reach, the roaring machines could not follow him. After a while he had felt safe enough to huddle down and sleep.

Now he uncurled and stretched. He was strangely stiff and sore. He remembered falling a long way, fighting a monster made of rocks and water. That should not have left such hurts. *What is wrong with me?*

Thirst tormented him. He spotted a puddle of rainwater gleaming in the hazy starlight. He crawled to it and drank. Tiny things were swimming in it and the water tasted of oil and dirt, but he was grateful.

Where will I go now? He crept forward to the low wall at the edge of the tower-top. He inched his head over the wall and peered out. Nothing moved below.

A little way from the base of this tower, many of those roaring machines stood in rows on the ground. Above them floated a crisscross of golden light, like a great star chained to the Earth. The machines were silent and lifeless now, perhaps harmless. Or perhaps not. They glittered menacingly under the shield of the golden star.

How far down was the ground? Suppose he fell from here? Suppose he threw himself down? But no, that would be a coward's act.

A warrior of the Urdar does not give up and die. He fights!

He stood up and faced into the wind. The cold bit into his body.

A warrior of the Urdar? Is that what I am? The thought warmed him.

Then he thought: *What is Urdar? Why can I not remember? This place is terrible. I want my home. I will fly from here.*

But he did not fly. He could not. He had no wings.

Wings! I had wings! And now I have none. Who has done this to me?

And where is home?

He crouched down against the stone fence and covered his face with the ugly, all-wrong hands. *Lost,* he wailed inside, where no enemy could hear. *Lost and cold and afraid.*

AMELIA WOKE. She lay a minute shivering and clutching the blankets to her chin. Her pillow was soaked with tears. For a moment she still heard his cry: *Lost!*

"Ty! Hold on, Ty. Hold on! I'm coming!"

Chapter 5

Shades of Lilac

"I'VE BEEN THINKING about our problem," Ike said on Saturday morning just before noon, as they waited for Amelia at the bus terminal. The intercity terminal in Dunstone was just a sign on a pole outside Smith's Hardware, on King Street. There was one bench, up against the store's front window, sheltered from the whistling north wind.

"Ammy is our problem." Simon huddled on the bench with his hands deep in his jacket pockets.

"No, no, that's the wrong way to look at it. Think of it like a gaming puzzle."

There were three world gates in Dunstone that they knew of, all leading to Mythrin. One was buried under tons of rock in a cave in the Dunn River gorge. One was a door in the air fifteen feet up, invisible and unreachable. And one stood behind the house of Lysander Manning, retired high school Latin and English teacher and Weird Games founder.

After that night last June, when a dragon had taken shape in Mr. Manning's back yard and the passage to another world opened in his rose arbour, he'd taken steps. The very next day he'd had a big steel shed built where the rose arbour used to be. He'd filled the shed with cement blocks, put a six-foot-high chain-link fence around the yard, and bought an oversized German shepherd named Bluto to live inside the fence. All that was meant to protect somebody, but Simon was

29

never sure who.

"Easy-peasy." Ike cracked his knuckles. "All we need is a few pounds of explosives to blow up the shed."

"Where would you get explosives?"

"You can get anything on the Internet, right?" Ike looked completely serious.

Simon shook his head. "Not a good idea."

"Then we'll have to talk Mr. Manning into letting us get at that gate. That'll be harder than getting dynamite."

The clock on the town hall tower struck twelve times for noon. The bus from Kitchener was late. Simon got up and squinted westward along the street. Ike tugged on the back of his jacket. "Heads up!"

Simon looked around. John Lilac was striding across the intersection towards them.

"He's looking at us," Ike whispered. "I think he wants to talk to us."

"I have lain sleepless," Lilac boomed, from halfway across the intersection. A car swerved to avoid him and beeped furiously. He ignored it. "I have cudgelled my brain."

"I, uh, I'm sorry to hear that," Simon said.

"Why is it I seem to know your face? Why do you smell so familiar?"

Smell? Simon wondered.

Lilac covered the last few yards in a few huge strides. He set a long hand on Simon's shoulder and steered him down onto the bench beside Ike. He sat down himself next to Simon. "I have remembered something. I know where first I saw your face."

"That's, um, that's great!" Simon wished there was more room on the bench. "You're starting to get your memory back!"

"Of that I am not so sure." Lilac's voice made the bench vibrate.

30

"I only know that I recall your face from a picture."

"A picture? But where—"

"As to where it was, I know not. As to when: the sight was among my earliest memories in this place. And it comes to me that it was a portent."

"A, um, portent?"

"A sign. A message."

"Oh." Simon eased away along the bench. Ike was about to fall off the end. "Uh, message about what?"

"Faith, boy, how would I know? If it was a portent, it was meant for you, not me!" John Lilac reached out a long forefinger and tapped Simon on the knee. "And so I have told you."

"Holy Hannah!" Ike whispered in Simon's ear. "Look at his hands!"

"My hands?" John Lilac held them out in front and spread his extra-jointed fingers with the blue nails. "My hands are well enough. Why do you fleer at them?" He surged to his feet. Simon and Ike jumped up and backed away.

"We didn't — I mean — it's okay!" Simon wanted to turn and run. At the same time he didn't want to hurt John Lilac's feelings. He smiled up at him. "It's okay, really."

"Why do you gaze at me so?"

"I, uh."

Ike pulled at his arm. "Simon! Come on!"

"Am I a monster, that you stare so?" Lilac stabbed a forefinger at Simon. "You gaze like a basilisk. Stop looking at me. *Stop seeing me!*"

Instantly Simon stopped seeing him — and everything else. Total darkness fell. He thought for a moment that he had shut his eyes. He tried opening them. Everything was still black.

I'm blind!

"Simon?" That was Ike. "What's the matter?"

Fear choked him. He couldn't make a sound.

Suddenly there was a tangle of voices around him. Ike's and a new voice, a man's: "Hey! Are you bothering these kids?"

A scurry of footsteps and another voice, a woman's, quick and angry: "Don't be stupid! He's not bothering anybody. You've upset him! You just leave him alone!"

The woman's voice turned soothing. It got fainter and fainter, as if she was moving away.

"Simon?" Ike sounded frightened.

Simon lifted a leaden hand and pushed it into his pocket. He curled his numb fingers around the Mythrin stone. That often helped when he was rattled. It helped now.

The blackness broke up into specks in front of his eyes. He blinked them away. Halfway across the intersection, a small dark-haired woman — Vesper Wynn — was leading John Lilac, or pushing him, or trying to hold him up, or all three.

Simon cleared his throat. "Wow." He let go of the stone but kept his hand in his pocket, just in case.

"Hey, are you all right?" The man was Wayne Smith, from the hardware store.

"Uh, yeah. I'm good. Thanks."

"That fella." Wayne shook his head. "I don't know. I just don't know." He went back into the store, still shaking his head.

"Here comes the bus," Ike said. "Only ten minutes late. Hey, what got into you? Looked like something whomped you over the head!"

But there was no time to tell Ike anything. The bus pulled up to the curb and the doors opened and Ammy jumped out, as if she had been camped in the aisle right behind the driver. "You guys!" she shouted. "I think I know where he is!"

AMELIA SHOVED her backpack at Simon, linked elbows with him and Ike, and dragged them along King Street to the town hall square. She sat them down on the curb of the fountain and told them about last night's dream.

"It was a true dream, a dragon dream," she said. "I could see and feel everything he saw and felt. Just like I was there! And guess where he was?"

Ike beamed back at her expectantly. Simon looked dazed.

"He was here!" She pointed up at the town hall tower, with the stone dragons carved under the parapet. "Up there, I mean. He got as high up as he could, and that's the highest place around, so it must've been up there."

"You're guessing," Ike said.

"Then he looked down at the street. Everything he saw looked awfully familiar. And there was one thing... If I'm right... C'mon!" She urged them up from the fountain and across the square and around the town hall onto Queen Street. And on the other side of the street.... "Yes! That's it! That's what he saw from the top of the tower!"

It was a used car lot. Strings of small lights, unlit now but glittering in the sunshine, outlined the lot and criss-crossed it from side to side and corner to corner.

"He saw a star shape." Amelia waved at it triumphantly. "He saw that!"

"I guess that means we won't have to go to Mythrin," Ike said. "Too bad. I had a foolproof plan for getting at that gate in Mr. Manning's yard. I even mapped it."

Amelia marvelled at him. *They're still just geeky little boys, especially Ike.* He'd been growing out his red hair and gelling it so it stuck up manga-style. And he wore high-top sneakers with silver

33

wings flying off the heels. But no amount of cool could cover up his basic geekiness.

Simon looked the same as ever. Oh, he'd grown taller in the last couple of months without getting any thinner. And he was quieter, if that was possible. But still — solid geek through and through.

"That's right, Ike." She spoke gently, as if to a child. "We don't need to go to Mythrin. We need to stay here and find Ty."

"Woo-hoo! Do we have a surprise for you!" He chortled and elbowed Simon.

Simon shook his head. "No way. Not the streaker."

"But the hair!"

"That was the only way they looked alike, the hair colour. Besides, he jumped in the gorge. How could he still be alive?"

"But," Ike began.

Amelia's hands itched to grab them and crack their heads together. She had to herd them into Bruce's Coffee and Doughnut and stuff them with chocolate glazeds to get the story, how the blue-haired streaker had appeared out of nowhere and raced across King Street and jumped into the gorge. Then she had to go and look into the gorge herself.

"That proves it," she said, turning away from the roar and the flying spray. "That's what he meant in the dream, when he thought about a monster made of rocks and water. Only a dragon could get out of that with just a few bruises."

They headed west on King Street. "But why would Ty freak out from being here in Dunstone?" Simon demanded. "He's been here before. And why would he look different?"

Amelia bit back her impatience. "Don't you get it? Dragons are shape changers, but he doesn't know what shape he should be. He doesn't know who he is. He doesn't even know he's a dragon! Something happened to knock him all sideways."

"And another thing. If he's Ty, how did he get here from Mythrin? You can't use any of the gates."

"Ha!" Ike bounced with excitement. "That gate by the library. *We* can't use it, but how about somebody coming the other way? He opens the gate okay, but then he comes out here, and splosh! down he goes into the gorge. Probably hit his head on a rock. That's why he'd do crazy things like running around naked in October."

Amelia pulled them to a stop outside Boomer Heaven. She gave each arm a shake. "I don't care how he got here! That's not important! Finding him, that's what important."

"And then what?" Simon asked mildly. "What are we going to do with a dragon who's lost his mind?"

"First things first. Find him. He'll be up high. Dragons like being in high places. He'll only feel safe up where he can see out over the town and nobody can look down on him."

Amelia dashed into Boomer Heaven to check in with Grandmother and get a hug. Then they went up to the apartment to find some clothes. That was Simon's idea, "In case he's still naked."

He had some extra-long jeans that he said might do. "He looked taller than me," Simon said. He stuffed those into a backpack along with some boxer shorts, warm woolen socks, a pair of heavy sandals that might fit because of the Velcro straps, and a thick fleece hoodie.

He was about to zip up the bag, then suddenly rooted around in the back of a drawer and pulled out an oversized red T-shirt. He stuffed that in the bag too.

"That's your DAWG T-shirt!" Ike tried to pull it out again. "You don't want to give that away!"

"Sure I do." Simon stuffed it back in and shouldered the bag. "Let's go dragon-hunting."

35

Chapter 6
Pigeon Feathers

"SO, HOW DO YOU like living in good ol' Hogtown?" Ike asked, as they clattered down the stairs to the lobby.

"Hate it," Ammy said, already pushing open the front door in that no-time-to-spare way she'd been wearing since she leaped off the bus.

"Toronto's wasted on you," Ike said. "It should've been me."

"Come on! How can we get up to the top of the town hall tower?"

"We can't," Simon said. "We've tried."

"Mrs. Quick is like the Mounties on Parliament Hill," Ike said.

"She's what, the front desk lady?" Ammy stopped in front of the *Dunstone Independent* office. "But you know how to get up there?"

"We know where the stairs to the roof are," Simon said cautiously. "But there's no way—"

"Okay, you can show me." She shoved her bangs back from her face with both hands. Her face looked older without a lot of hair hanging in her eyes. Older and stubborn as a rock. "Here's what we'll do. Ike, you'll keep Mrs. Quick busy while Simon takes me up to the roof."

"Keep her busy how?"

"I don't know! Tell her jokes. Take her picture. Say it's a school assign—"

"Yes!" Ike waved a fist. "Brilliant! We'll use the power of the

36

press!"

"The what?" Ammy frowned at Simon, as if he was to blame for Ike.

"The power of the press," Ike repeated grandly. "I'll borrow my dad's camera with the wide-angle lens. I'll say the *Independent* wants to run a huge front-page shot of the town, taken from the roof, showing how much it's grown. She'll love it!" He straight-armed through the *Independent's* glass door.

"It'll never work," Simon said. "He wrecked his new camera last winter when we fell out of that world gate, remember? His father won't ever let him borrow his."

"Besides, she'll want to know why Ike's doing it and not Oscar."

Something moving high above the street caught Simon's eye. It was pigeons, a big flock of them, swirling and circling above the roofs. Most of the flock settled on the flat-topped bell tower of Emmanuel Lutheran Church at the corner of King and Dunning, a block west of the Hammer Building.

From here you could see just the front face of the yellowy-grey brick tower. Its tall, narrow windows were covered with slanted slats instead of glass. Pigeons sidled in and out from between the slats on one of the windows, but not the others.

"Look." He pointed out the bell tower to Ammy. "You ever think how many pigeons there must be in a town? I bet there's more pigeons than people."

As soon as he said that, the tower exploded. Or that's how it looked. There was a furious drumming of wings and pigeons poured out of the window.

"What's got into them?" Ammy glowered upward.

"Somebody must be up there in the tower. Scaring them."

They looked at each other. Ammy's gaze went inward, remembering. "He was thirsty last night," she murmured. "He must be hungry by now."

Simon dashed inside the *Independent's* office. Ike was hanging over his father's computer, talking at top speed. Simon grabbed his arm and hauled him away. "It's okay, we don't need the camera!"

Oscar stared after them. "What's going on?"

Simon waved desperately and pushed Ike, who was yelping protests, out the door. Ammy was already halfway along the block towards the church. "We won't need your camera," Simon puffed. "Somehow — I don't think the — power of the — press — is going to get us up — that bell tower!"

"HELP ME understand this," said Pastor Helmut Grimm. "You want to visit my bell chamber. All by yourselves. Because you think a mentally disturbed person might be hiding up there."

"That's right." Amelia tried on a disarming smile. "Please," she added, as sweetly as she knew how.

"Why on Earth would I let you do something so dangerous?"

He leaned against the closed door at the back of the porch that led to the tower stairs, and waited. Pastor Grimm was nothing like his name — he was young and rather nice-looking, Amelia thought, and he smiled easily. But something about that smile said that the Pastor was good at seeing through flimflam.

She dropped the cute look. "He's a friend. If the police get to him first he'll fight them again, and then he might get shot."

"I don't think our police would shoot him."

"Well, he might get hurt. But just let us up there and we can talk him down. Because he'll know us."

"Maybe," Ike put in.

Ammy wanted to kick him. "His name is Ty. Ty, uh, Jones. We met him last summer. He's from out of town."

Simon opened his pack and pulled out the boxer shorts. "We

38

brought clothes for him. He must be cold up there."

Pastor Grimm nodded. "Good thinking. All right, let's go and see." (Strange, Amelia thought, how the boxer shorts convinced him.) He opened the door and started up the narrow spiral stairs.

"Oh, but you don't need to come. We can—" Ammy began. He cut her off cheerfully.

"If somebody's living in my bell tower, I want to know who!"

The stairs led to a second-floor room that was bare except for a set of thick ropes that came down from holes in the ceiling and were tied up to hooks in the walls.

"Where are the bells?" Ike looked around and up at the ceiling. "Up there? Can I—" He reached for a rope.

"No," said Pastor Grimm.

Amelia and Simon pulled Ike towards a ladder on the wall, where Pastor Grimm was already starting up. Amelia grabbed the rungs under Grimm's feet and started up after him.

At the top of the ladder he pushed open a trap door in the ceiling. He turned cautiously, and went still. They could see him watching something. Amelia trembled. "Don't scare him!" she whispered.

"Hello there, my friend," said Pastor Grimm, in the sort of voice you'd use to calm a frightened dog. "Easy, now. It's all right." He climbed up a few more rungs and stepped out on the floor above. "I have some of your pals here. They've come to see if you're okay."

As soon as Amelia's head was above the level of the trap door she twisted around. "Uhn." Her heart felt like a chunk of lead.

Simon was right. This guy looked nothing like the Ty she knew — the tall, proud, mohawk-crested warrior with the cat-slit golden eyes and the sharp-toothed grin. The only thing those two had in common was bright blue-green hair, but with this guy it was a wild mop that hung over his face.

The man — no, the boy, you could see that now, he was eighteen at most — was sitting on the dusty, feathery floor with his back to the brick wall, next to one of the slatted windows. Several of the slats were broken off, enough to make a hole big enough for him to climb through. Wire mesh on the inside had been pushed aside, which, she guessed, was how the pigeons had got in. The mesh on the other windows was still attached.

The boy was covered with grey pigeon feathers. Feathers stuck out of his hair, sat in heaps on his shoulders, and clung to his chest and legs.

"Hoo, is this place ever a dump!" said Ike, who had wormed his way up past Simon and Amelia and now stood near the trap door. He looked around. "Way cool!"

The bells weren't hanging from the ceiling, which surprised Amelia. They sat in a complicated frame of thick wooden beams and metal wheels as big as themselves. The frame and bells took up half the floor space.

But she barely glanced at them. The boy sitting on the floor was too important. He seemed to have a lap full of feathers. She wondered why, until he lifted something in his hands and gnawed at it.

"Oh, yuck!" Ike made a gagging sound.

The boy had caught a pigeon and was eating it. Raw! He stared at Ike and then at Pastor Grimm, who was moving towards him step by cautious step, holding out a hand and making soothing noises. Still gnawing at the pigeon, the boy eased himself up the stone wall and closer to the hole in the slats.

Oh! He really is naked! Amelia shut her eyes.

"Now that's a funny thing," Simon said, as if to himself. "He must've got in by that window. That means he climbed the tower from the outside. So...."

Amelia opened her eyes. The boy was staring at Simon now. He flapped the pigeon at him. "You," he said, in a scratchy voice that

40

was not Ty's. "You face."

"You know me?" Simon pushed Amelia up onto the floor and climbed out past her.

"No. Yes." The boy scooted closer to the hole in the slats.

"Ty!" Amelia called. She couldn't help herself, the name just slipped out. "Ty, it's me! Amelia!" She climbed to her feet and held out both hands.

He looked at her, finally. All she could see was a gleam of eyes through a blue-green tangle. Then something flashed in her head, and she knew, the same way she knew her own face in the mirror. "It's him!" She did a little dance for sheer joy and stirred up a cloud of dust and feathers.

Ty grinned. His teeth were white and even, and not pointed. There was nothing dragonish about him at all, except maybe that hair colour. And who knew, maybe that wasn't real. Maybe he'd got into a tube of blue-green hair gel at the mall.

It didn't matter. *I'd know him if he was shaped like a, a porcupine!*

"We need to get him away from that window," Grimm said quietly.

"Look, Ty." Simon opened his backpack and pulled clothes out of it. "These are for you."

"No." Ty waved them away with the half-eaten pigeon.

"You need to wear clothes, Ty." Amelia took a step closer, still holding his eyes. "So they won't chase you."

Ty glanced towards the street. "Chase." He chuckled rustily. "Fun."

Now, that sounded like Ty. "Yes. But if they catch you it won't be fun."

"No?"

"No. But if you put on these clothes, you'll look like him." She

41

pointed at Simon, who was holding up the boxer shorts invitingly. "He's a friend."

A voice murmured up through the trap door. "My caretaker," said Pastor Grimm. He bent over the hole. "All right so far. But you should…." He mimed a telephone with his hand.

"Not the police!" Amelia whispered.

"They have training for situations like this." He patted her arm. "It's the best thing, I promise."

"But he's not crazy! He's just — not himself."

"Of course." He wasn't listening. He was moving slowly around the outside of the bell frame towards Ty, picking up the pair of socks in passing.

Maybe it will be all right, Amelia thought. She stood clenching her hands with worry.

For a few minutes it did seem as if Ty had been tamed. He let Grimm and Simon and Ike help him into the clothes, although it wasn't easy, because he wouldn't let go of the pigeon. He seemed to like the bright red DAWG shirt, wanting to hold it over his eyes and look at the light through it. Everything was a little short on him, even the jeans, but they were better than nothing.

The only things he didn't like were the socks and sandals. After they were on he took a few steps, wiggled his feet, and then sat down and tore them off. Simon shrugged and stuffed them back in his pack. "I guess he likes to keep his toes free for climbing," he said.

Pastor Grimm had manoeuvred himself around behind Ty so that he blocked the broken window. Then he seemed to realize. He looked at Simon. "You think he climbed?" He looked at the hole in the slats. "From outside? But surely not! How could anyone—"

Ty isn't just anyone, Amelia was about to tell him, but she never did. Just at that moment there came the sound of footsteps on the floor below, and then the scuff of boot soles on the rungs of the ladder, and then a familiar face appeared in the square of the trap door. Constable Lisa Nader. She had left her OPP peaked hat below.

"How are things here?" She stayed where she was and smiled at Ty. "Are you okay? Ready to come down?"

Ty leaped up. He backed towards the window, smack into Pastor Grimm, who tried to hold him. Ty pushed him aside. Grimm sprawled. "Ty, wait!" Amelia bounced forward. "Ty, it's all right!"

Lisa Nader was out of the trap door and around the bell frame like a ferret, shouldering Amelia aside. But Ty was quicker. He shot a laughing look at Amelia. "You wrong!" He poured himself through the hole and was gone.

Lisa was instantly on her way back to the ladder, cell phone clapped to her ear, calling for an ambulance. By the time they reached the bottom of the tower and had run out to the street, a small crowd had gathered. Lisa and the Pastor pushed through. Amelia knew what they expected to find: Ty all in bits on the sidewalk.

"Won't they be surprised," Simon said. Ike laughed.

Amelia didn't feel like laughing. You *wrong, he said. He thinks I lied to him.*

Ty wasn't there. People were bending over Lisa's partner, Constable Bob Lebrun, who was sitting on the ground holding his jaw. "That kid has a heck of a right hook," he said, and winced.

Oscar arrived, uncasing his camera. He took a shot of Lebrun being helped to his feet.

"I've never seen anything like it," said Mrs. Miriam Schweter, who had been crossing the street on her way to the church, her arms full of flowers for tomorrow's services, when it all happened. "He came down that wall head-first, like a lizard. You know, like he had suction cups on his toes. He was holding a pigeon in his teeth by one wing."

"Well," Simon said, "now at least he's dressed."

Chapter 7

Questions, Questions

IT WAS HALF AN HOUR before they could get away. The police took them back into the church porch and sat them down on hard chairs and asked dozens of questions: how they knew this guy, and why they were helping him, and where he came from. So did Oscar.

Everybody remembered the tall punk who'd teamed up with Ammy at the Weird Games in June. "He had blue hair then too," Lisa Nader said. "And he came out of nowhere, just like now. Well, now we have a name. Ty Jones. That should help track him down."

"A photo would help," said Lebrun, who still winced when he talked. "Oscar?"

"Sorry. I tried at the games, but I never could photograph that guy. Strangest thing I've ever come across." Oscar stared thoughtfully at Ike and Simon, than Amelia. Ike squirmed on his chair and looked as if he was hiding the evidence for a dozen guilty secrets in his back pockets.

"Like a lizard with suction cups on his toes!" Lisa laughed. "The things people say!"

"Still, this guy's out of the ordinary, no doubt about it," Oscar said. "He survived his fall into the gorge, for one thing. And did you kids know they haven't found his clothes? It's like he just popped out of thin air."

Simon smiled nervously. If anybody could figure out the truth without freaking, he thought, it would probably be Oscar.

Lisa let them go, finally. "But remember, you're not to approach him." She looked hard at Ammy. "If you see him, call us. Don't go near him! He could be dangerous. Okay?"

Ammy mumbled something. Lisa shook her head. "For Pete's sake, Amelia, we won't hurt him! We want to help him. Just leave him to us!"

"DUNSTONE Heritage Lanes?" Ammy looked up, amazed, at the mall's new facade. The glass-and-steel front entrance was now surrounded by huge, grey, weathered stones. "What's that mean?"

They'd decided to go to the mall to plan their next move. Maybe they'd get some clue about how Ty got here, Ike said, because the mall was where people saw him first.

Simon explained about the heritage theme. "They got some old stones that were stored from the building that used to be here. Heritage *anything* is supposed to bring in crowds of tourists."

"It doesn't look very crowded," Ammy said, as they passed the front escalators. "And why is it so dark?"

"That's all the wood," Ike said. Dark brown wooden planks and shingles covered the storefronts and framed the doors and windows. "It's like a pioneer village street."

"With harp music?" Ammy tilted her head and listened. "Brutal!"

They stopped in a rustic doorway and looked in. A woman sat in front of a big, complicated wooden machine with parts that clacked and swung. "This used to be Eleganz." Ammy frowned. "What happened to the stores?"

"These are all real old-type workshops," Simon said. "There was a piece about it in the *Independent* a while back. See, she's weaving." The woman nodded and smiled. They smiled back and walked on. "You can watch her weave and then you can buy handmade blankets and things."

"How exciting," Ammy half-lidded her eyes.

"There's a glassblower," Ike said. "That one's kind of fun."

They stopped to watch the glassblower making round ornaments out of molten glass. Next to him there was a silversmith, and farther on they passed a potter, a book binder, a quilter, a bowyer-fletcher (hunting bows and arrows), an apothecary ("Drug store with extra herbs," Ike said), and two women who made uncomfortable-looking chairs out of twigs.

There were regular stores too, like Doogie's Shoes and Wired Zone Electronics, on the opposite corridor. But most of the mall was pioneer-style now.

"They're like fish in fishbowls." Ike backed away from the twiggers, who looked ready to come out and drag them inside. "Piranhas, maybe."

"I feel sorry for them," Simon said.

"It's so depressing!" Ammy hunched her shoulders and shivered. "I used to like this mall."

"The food court is still okay, in spots," Ike said. "Only they don't call it that now. They call it the Pioneer Emporium."

You couldn't get pizza or Chinese food here any more. You could buy sandwiches from the butcher shop and "harvest soup" from the greengrocer. (Ammy made a disgusted sound.) The Espresso Bar, with the shiny brass eagle on top of the espresso machine, was gone. There was a tea shop in its place, run by two ladies in long print dresses and frilly aprons. (Ammy rolled up her eyes.)

You could still get cinnamon buns and hot chocolate, but you had to eat and drink them at wooden tables inside a stone ruin in the middle of the food court, lit by a skylight two storeys above. The stones looked old but the rebuilt ruin looked new. "And fake," Ammy said.

They were almost the only people in the Pioneer Emporium.

Dinisha Rajeev and a couple of her girlfriends had their heads together at another table.

"More of the old stones, right?" Ammy pointed at the rough, roofless walls that rose nearly to the level of the mezzanine balcony. "Where did you say they came from?"

"Some old jail or school or something," Ike said.

"Jail, I bet." Ammy gulped down her hot chocolate. "This place is just like that. And that harp music is driving me crazy. Let's find out what we can and get out."

Seeing two men in work clothes who were fitting a new sheet of glass in the butcher shop window, Ammy went over, half-eaten cinnamon bun in hand, to ask how the window got broken.

"You didn't hear? There was this wild man, yesterday, with blue hair," said one of the workers. "This is the third window we've fixed."

Ammy went back to the table. "Looks like Ty was here, all right. Somebody must have seen where he came from! I'm going to keep asking 'til I get an answer."

"We'll split up," Simon said. He started at the tea shop. The ladies smiled at him, but the smiles soon vanished. "We were told not to say anything to anybody," said one. "Since it's still a police investigation," said the other.

"Um, okay. Thanks." He moved on to the greengrocer. The man at the cash just shook his head. It didn't take long to canvass the whole food court. Ten minutes later they met near the rear escalator. Nobody would answer any questions.

"They're all afraid of the mall cops!" Ike said. "The guy in the cheese shop told me. The security guys told them not to talk about the streaker because it would scare shoppers away."

"So they'll get bored to death, instead." Ammy looked around for a trash bin to throw away the last scrap of her cinnamon bun. She glanced over Simon's shoulder. Her eyes widened. "I don't ... believe ... this!"

Simon turned around. For a moment he thought something had happened to his eyes again. Only this time, instead of being struck blind, he was seeing in sixes. Ike let out a snort of laughter.

"Kevin?" Ammy bit her lip. "Is that you?"

Kevin stamped to a halt with the quints lined up behind him. The six of them were dressed in identical grey hoodies, each with a peel-and-press name tag stuck to the right shoulder. PEER MONITOR # 1, said Kevin's name tag. The others were peer monitors # 2, 3, 4, 5, and 6.

They all wore mirrored sunglasses. They all had their hair buzzed so short they looked bald. Somebody at Simon's elbow let out a squeal. "Kevin!" It was Dinisha. "You look—" She pressed both hands over her mouth.

Kevin swaggered, thumbs in his jeans pockets. "You like it?"

"No! It's horrible! Your *hair*!"

"It's part of the look."

"But you all look alike!"

"That's the idea. We've volunteered as Dunstone Heritage Lanes peer monitors. I'm the peer monitor captain." He jerked a thumb over his shoulder. "They're constables."

"Peer monitor," Simon repeated. "So, what do you do?"

"We keep an eye on people our own age in the mall — I mean the Heritage Lanes — and report any signs of trouble. Like, you three." Kevin slipped a small notebook and pen from his hoodie pocket. He wrote something in it and then pointed the pen at Ammy. "You can't take food outside the pioneer garden eating area. That's against the rules."

"Oh, spare me!" Ammy spotted a trash bin just outside the rebuilt ruin and tossed the bun at it. It missed and bounced over the floor.

48

"Oops!"

"See, that's what I mean." Kevin made another note. "I think you'd better leave now, before you get in real trouble." He pocketed the notebook and set hands on hips.

"But Kevin, why?" demanded Dinisha. "I mean, why are you doing this — this peer pressure stuff?"

"Peer *monitor*. Don't you think it's a good idea?" He looked puzzled. "I'm planning on a career in police someday, or maybe army. You know that. This will help me with my policing skills."

"Me too," said one of the quints. The others nodded.

Ike, who had been standing behind Simon and snickering quietly, chose that moment to leap forward. "My gosh! You've done it! You've made scientific history! Let me shake your hand!" He grabbed Kevin's hand and pumped it up and down.

Kevin pulled free. "What for?" He narrowed his eyes.

Uh-oh. Simon stepped forward, but too late.

"What for?" Ike was up on his toes with amazement. "What *for*? You're the first person in history ever to clone himself — not once but five times! That's so awesome! I am truly humbled to — Wait a minute." He stared from face to face. "Which one is the original Kevin? Which are the clones?" He clutched at his hair. "Oh no! How will we ever tell? What if you get your labels mixed up?"

"Did he just call us clowns?" one of the quints asked another.

Kevin's face was turning red. He pulled a cell phone from a leather holster on his belt and punched in a number. "Peer monitor one. Food court."

"You've gotta be kidding!" Dinisha laughed. Kevin walked away towards the shops corridor, muttering into his phone. The quints marched after him.

"That's so not cool," said one of Dinisha's girlfriends. The other giggled.

"What's got into Kevin?" Ammy asked. "He used to be just a jerk. Now he's a super-jerk."

Dinisha shook her head. "He's not, really." She watched Kevin hang a sharp right and disappear around the corner. Simon thought: *She looks sad. She really likes him. But why?*

"Kevin's changed, just these last couple of weeks," she said. "All he wants to do now is hang at the mall and pretend to be a security guard. Like they're his heroes. Well, I'm not wasting my time here any more."

Dinisha and her friends headed out the rear door to the parking lot on Queen Street. "I think we better go too," Simon said.

"Before the mall cadets come back, you mean?" Ike snorted.

"Too late!" Ammy nodded past him. "And he's got backup."

Kevin and the quints were back, tagging at the heels of the two massive security guards. They stopped at the east entrance to the food court and stood aside to let a small man in a suit and tie step out in front. "Who's that?" Ammy asked.

"The manager, I think." Simon got up from the table and dropped the last of their trash into the bin. "Let's go." Kevin was pointing across the court at them and then pointing at his open notebook. The man stared at them with hard little black eyes set close on either side of a long, sharp nose. When he saw them looking, his front teeth showed through a short, bristly moustache. It didn't look like a smile.

"Those guards are burning holes in me with their eyes," Ike said. "Let's clear out before we get kicked out."

The guards were starting to move in their direction. "This way!" Simon headed out the food court's west exit and around the curving corridor, a mirror image of the one they'd come in by.

He stopped to take his usual quick look into Doogie's Shoes, which stood next to the Wired Zone. He'd been checking the store window every week. Good: still no shoes with stars on the ankles. If

50

they ever turned up, this would be the place.

"They're coming!" Ike said. Ammy and Ike each took one of Simon's arms and rushed him into the shop and into a corner, where they couldn't be spotted from the corridor. A middle-aged woman in black, with a startling topknot of stiff sulfur-yellow hair, dropped a stack of shoe boxes on the floor and stared at them in amazement.

Heavy feet tramped past outside, followed by a scurry of sneakers (guards, then Kevin and the quints, Simon thought), and then a pattering sound, like animal feet trotting. The pattering stopped in the doorway. "Ah, Miss Dogood," someone said in a high voice.

"That's my name, don't wear it out." She strolled to the doorway.

"Have you seen two boys and a girl, perhaps thirteen years old? Mischief-makers! Vandals!"

"I've seen nobody of that description, Mr. Ralston. So sorry!"

The feet pattered away. Miss Dogood moved back into view. "It's safe to come out, kids."

"Hey, thanks!" Ammy said.

Miss Dogood shrugged. "I see Harry had all the troops out. What on Earth did you do?"

"Made fun of the peer monitors." Ike smirked.

"Shocking!"

"And dropped a cinnamon bun," Ammy added. "Not on purpose." She picked up a purple suede boot and sighed over it.

"And you?" Miss Dogood looked at Simon. "Wait, I know you. You're Celeste Hammer's grandson, right? You're the boy who keeps coming to look in my window."

"I, um, yes."

"Well, you'll be happy to know that I'm planning a closing sale. Starting next week — everything 40 per cent off! Including some great new stock I just got in. Come back Monday and tell all your friends!"

"Oh, we will," Ike said. "But why are you closing?"

"I'm moving back to my little old shop at Queen and Dunning. Nothing's working out here. They said we'd all do a booming business, but the customers just aren't coming. Even the vending machines don't work properly." She lowered her voice and beckoned them closer. "You won't believe this, but it's true. I saw it myself. One of them was dispensing centipedes!"

"Yikes!" Ammy nearly dropped the suede boot.

"Yes, and each centipede was wrapped up like a tiny chocolate bar!"

Ammy looked at the price on the boot, grimaced, and put it back. "Miss Dogood? Were you here yesterday when there was all the excitement?"

"Was I!" Miss Dogood laughed. "Oh my! I was in the food court and suddenly there he was. Riding up on the escalator. Not on the step. He was standing on the rubber handrail, of all things!"

"You mean he came up from the lower level?" Simon asked. "Did he have his clothes on then?"

"No! He was starkers! They say he must have taken off his clothes down there, but I don't think they ever found any. Maybe he left them in the caves!"

"Caves?" said Simon and Ammy and Ike in chorus.

"I never heard about any caves under the mall," Simon said.

"Me neither," Ike said. "And we've both lived here all our lives."

"Well, maybe it's all lies on Harry's part. I mean Harry Ralston, the building manager. The one who tried to sniff you out just now. Harry keeps saying how historic and special this mall is. But I wouldn't know, I'm not a local gal myself."

"Caves!" Simon exchanged excited looks with Ike and Ammy. "Who would know?"

"You could go talk to Lysander Manning. He helps Vesper Wynn run the bookstore. He can tell you all about the town and its history."

Ike went to the door and peered out. "I think the coast is clear. We can get to the front door if we make a run for it."

Simon was the last one out. "Miss Dogood? I hope your sale goes well. And, um, thanks again. For not telling Mr. Ralston we were here."

She waved a hand. "Think nothing of it. I never did like that man."

Chapter 8

Seeking

THEY SPENT the rest of the afternoon searching for Ty. Simon got his binoculars and they climbed to the top of Founders Tower, the landmark on the ridge above Dunstone, to scan the rooftops below.

They never saw Ty. But they did see Lisa Nader and Bob Lebrun on the top of the town hall tower, looking at marks in the gravel. And someone was hammering fresh slats on the windows of the Lutheran bell tower. They also caught a glimpse of John Lilac on the roof of the used bookstore, prowling back and forth.

"I wish I could talk to him properly," Simon said. "Now that I think of it, there are some things about him that make me think of Ty. Like, he came out of nowhere, and he didn't know who he was. He still doesn't."

"Wait a minute." Ike lowered the binoculars. "You think maybe John Lilac could be a dragon too?"

Simon shook his head. "I never heard of a dragon like him. The way he talks! And he reads all these books. I never heard of Mara or any of the other dragons reading books."

"I don't think they even have real writing," Ammy said.

"But if he's not a dragon," Ike persisted, "then what is he?"

Simon shrugged. "Some other kind of alien. Think about it. Maybe they didn't come direct from Mythrin. Maybe Ty was exploring and he got into another world, Lilac's world. And they both came to Earth from there. We already know there are lots of gates, not just the ones between Earth and Mythrin, right?"

"Ty was scouting them out, last I heard," Ammy said.

"There you go." Simon nodded. "And there's something else." He told them what happened outside the bookstore Friday afternoon, when Kevin and the quints were playing catch with his library book. And John Lilac came out and shouted *Cease!* And everything stopped, or seemed to.

"And this morning, at the bus stop, remember? He didn't want me staring at him. He said, *Stop seeing me!* And, and," this bit still made him shake, "and suddenly I couldn't see anything. For I don't know how long. Until I touched the Mythrin stone."

"The Mythrin stone," Ammy said thoughtfully. "Let's have a look."

Simon brought it out and held it on his palm.

"Remember what we found out?" Ike touched the dark red star. "The word dragon means 'to see clearly.' You must've touched the blood spot. That's what did it."

Ammy took the stone, held it tight and moved her gaze back and forth over the town below. She shook her head and handed it back. "No good."

"Maybe it's not that kind of seeing it means," Simon said.

"Well, that doesn't help us now." Ammy leaned on the railing. "If only I could fly! I don't know why I can fly on Mythrin but not here, on Earth. If I could, I'd be sure to spot him."

"If you could fly," Simon said, "you'd have to be a dragon first. You wouldn't last five minutes as a dragon. Somebody would shoot you down."

They waited until late that evening before walking over to Dunn River Books. "If it's not busy," Ammy said, "there's less chance we'll get brushed off." When they filed quietly into the store at eight, only a couple of customers wandered among the shelves.

Mr. Manning sat on a high stool behind the front desk. He was the only person in Dunstone, Simon thought, who would wear a suit and tie on Saturday. He had switched from summer whites to a dark tweed suit for fall, but still wore his bright red DAWG tie, with the cartoon of a goofy-looking hound on it.

"Welcome to our establishment!" Mr. Manning swept out a long arm. "How may I help you?"

"We have some questions about the mall," Simon said. "I mean, about what's under it." He repeated what Miss Dogood had told them.

Mr. Manning listened intently. Then he said. "Hmh. You know, I never thought it was a good idea to build a mall, or anything else, on that site. Still less to use those stones!"

"They came from an old building that used to be there, right?" Ike put in. "They're heritage. People keep saying we should be proud of our heritage."

"Not all of it!"

"Why?" Ammy demanded. "What was there before?"

"There's a book on it. Let me see…" Mr. Manning drummed his fingers on the counter a moment, then unfolded himself from the stool and went into the back of the store. A minute later he was back with a big, flat book under his arm. He held it up in both hands.

"*Corrective Institutions in Ontario, 1850 – 1950*," Ammy read aloud. "Urg. Sounds deadly!" She shrugged at him. "Sorry. But it does."

"The book is actually quite interesting." Mr. Manning set it on the front desk and opened it. "The subject is what's deadly. Here. Have a gander." He tapped a black-and-white photo that took up most of a two-page spread. They bent over it.

"Gosh!" Ike said.

"Dunstone County Gaol," Ammy read. "Gay-ol?"

"It's pronounced 'jail'," Mr. Manning said. "And that's what it means."

Simon said nothing. He felt cold. The picture showed a five-storey stone building that seemed to cover most of a city block, judging by the size of the tiny people standing next to it. Huge blocks of stone jutted out at the corners and along the roof, casting dark shadows down the sides. The walls were blank except for a few narrow windows like squinting eyes.

The picture was taken from the bottom of a flight of stairs that started behind heavy iron gates set between two massive pillars. It climbed to a castle-sized front door set deep under an arch of stone. From this angle the building seemed to tower up and lean over you. Simon felt like taking a step back.

"Wow," Ammy said. "A sight of that would be enough to scare anybody out of a life of crime!"

"No doubt that was the idea." Mr. Manning turned the page. Here were some photographs taken about 1900, a few years before the jail was closed down, he said. One photo showed a group of men in fur hats and coats with fur collars, standing between snowbanks in front of the iron gate. "There's the jail governor," Mr. Manning began, and then Ike's finger poked down.

"Hey! Isn't that—?" Ike took away his finger and tried to get his head down to the page. "Nah. Couldn't be."

"Try this." Mr. Manning held out a large magnifying glass.

Ike took it and held it over the photo. "Yowsers. Who's that?" He pointed. "That guy on the left end of the other guys, in a uniform."

Ammy grabbed the glass and squinted. "It's Harry Ralston!"

"Can't be." Simon got a look through the lens, finally. He blinked. The man sure did look like Harry, right down to the pointy nose, bristly moustache and hard little black eyes. He was taller than Harry, but that was the only difference.

57

"If you had troubled to read the caption," Mr. Manning said dryly.

"Oh." Simon read it. "Whole bunch of names, and… 'Cornelius Ralston, chief warder.'"

"That would be Harry Ralston's great-grandfather. Warder means guard. Harry likes to boast that his great-grandfather was chief warder in the jail and his grandfather a watchman in the school that followed it. Personally, I wouldn't think it a matter for boasting." He closed the book and pushed it away from him on the counter.

"Great!" Ammy grabbed the book and started leafing through it. "Now we need to know about caves. Like, what caves there are in the gorge and especially near the mall."

"Please?" Simon added, since Ammy seemed to have ditched her manners. "It's important."

Mr. Manning went off muttering something that sounded like *geomorphology*.

While they were waiting, Vesper Wynn strode from the back of the store and whisked behind the counter. She always walked as if she was angry at the ground under her feet. She'd be nice-looking, Simon thought, with those big, dark eyes, if only she could let go of the frown lines between her eyebrows.

"Well?" Vesper skewered Ammy with a look. "Do you plan to buy that book or not?"

Ammy's face went pink. "Haven't decided yet," she said loftily. She went back to turning the pages, only now extra slowly.

Vesper's frown lines deepened. Just give Ammy time, Simon thought, she'll get us tossed out. "Uh, how is Mr. Lilac? Is he okay?"

"No, he is not okay!" Vesper's eyes shone with anger. "Whatever you said to him this morning, it upset him terribly. He's almost back to what he was like when he came! He's been up on the roof most of the day talking to himself." She twisted around on the stool to look out the window at the street, shaking her head as if she'd said too much.

"What does he say?" Ammy clapped the book shut. "Is he speaking English?"

Vesper spun back. "What business is that of yours?"

"We have a friend who might be…" Ammy thought about how to put it.

"Who might've come from the same place," Simon finished for her.

"Well, perhaps might have," Ike put in, from behind a display of hologram bookmarks. "It's those hands, you know."

"He can't help his hands." Vesper slipped down from the stool, which left her no taller than Ammy. "I think you kids better leave."

"It's not the hands, not really," Simon said quickly. "It's … I think he's special."

She looked at him, the frown lines deeper than ever.

"I think he . . . he can do things." He talked faster, not sure how much time she'd give him. "Make things happen with just his voice. He's good, too, he stops bullies." He looked hopefully at Vesper. The frown lines had smoothed out between her eyes, but she still wasn't smiling. "Um, I heard you were the first person to see him. Where was that?"

She held his eyes. "I'd say you kids were pulling my leg really hard—"

"No!" Ammy broke in, but Vesper held up both palms.

"I'd say that, only I've seen . . . felt . . . some . . . *things* myself. Yes, he is . . . special. Different."

Not human. The words shimmered in the air between them, but nobody said them, not even Ike. Simon had a feeling Vesper would flip back to being angry if anyone said them.

"This building backs on the gorge," she said. "I was up on the

59

roof one day last summer and I looked down and there he was. Crouched next to a rock. He looked miserable, so I went down and got him out."

"In the gorge!" Ike bounced. "Naked?"

She sliced a frown at him. "Yes. And cold and scared. I called a friend and we went down and rescued him. Got him into some clothes. Talked him into going to a hospital."

"Could he talk?" Ammy asked.

"Not at first. But he picked up language amazingly fast. He's extremely intelligent, you know. He's just been *inhaling* books." A little pink came into her pale cheeks. "The doctors can't do a thing for him, but who knows, maybe someday I can help him get his memory back. Anyway, he's happy with me." She twitched her eyebrows at Simon. "Or would be, if people would leave him alone!"

"I think maybe," Simon began. He was going to tell her Lilac had remembered something this morning, but Vesper seemed to have had enough of them.

She looked over their heads. "Oh, good. Lysander." She sidestepped past them and hurried to the back of the store. Footsteps ran up the stairs.

Mr. Manning walked around to the back of the desk and thumped down another book, this one thick, dark blue and dusty. "It took some searching, but I found something relevant. Now — have you got what you want?" He beamed at them.

"Oh, you bet! Thanks!" Simon looked inside the covers of both books. "How much will these cost?" He looked again. "Ouch!"

"Call them loaners," Mr. Manning said. "Just bring them back in the same condition, mm?" He tapped a finger on his lips. "Don't tell Vesper!"

Chapter 9

The Mystery of Dunstone Gaol

THEY CARRIED the books back to Simon's room in the apartment. Simon and Ike sat on the floor against the side of the bed while Ammy sprawled on the coverlet with her chin on her arms.

They picked their way first through the thick, dusty book, finding the bits about the Dunstone area. There was a lot about how the gorge had been shaped at the end of the last ice age by rivers cutting their way down through the limestone bedrock. Caves formed along cracks, where water seeped down and slowly dissolved the limestone. Nobody knew how many caves there were. Most of the known ones were small and shallow.

"That doesn't tell us a lot," Ammy grumbled.

"It tells us there *could* be more caves people don't know about, and they *could* be under the part of Dunstone where the mall is," Simon said. "And that means—"

"There could be a world gate under there!" Ike pumped his fists. "Yes! That would explain so much!"

"'Could be' doesn't help." Ammy yawned. "We need a map!"

Simon pulled the other book over and opened it across his knees. The picture of the Dunstone County Gaol hit him again like a blast of cold air.

Those tiny windows were barred, he saw now. He wondered what the rooms behind them were like. He flipped the page quickly.

"Wait, let's see that!" Ike pulled the book over and read: "'Built in 1860, the Dunstone County Gaol was intended to be the finest example of modern corrections. Unlike earlier prisons, it was designed to separate men from women, adult prisoners from children (*Children! Ammy echoed*), and minor offenders from murderers and the mentally ill. Unfortunately, none of these provisions were carried out. As many as 500 prisoners were forced to share fewer than 200 cells, some no larger than one by two metres. The Gaol was closed in 1905 after an investigation revealed a long history of cruelty and violence by both the guards and the prisoners.'"

"Caves, Ike!" Ammy knuckled the top of his head. "Isn't there anything in there about caves underneath the prison?"

He turned a few more pages. "Doesn't look like it."

"So, close it up. I'm tired, I've had a long day. I don't want to have nightmares too."

"You can see why Mr. Manning thinks they should've left those stones alone," Simon said.

"You're not kidding." Ike went on turning pages. "Yikes, you should see what some of those cells looked like." He looked up, wide-eyed. "Now, here's something interesting. There was a mysterious hidden chamber in the jail! It says here, 'The guards softened up hard cases by putting them in Buckingham Palace. This was their name for a special cell marked by complete darkness and silence. Prisoners were stripped and held there, sometimes for weeks, with no light, no heat even in the coldest weather, and the bare minimum of water and bread. Strangely, in 1975, when the building was demolished and the stone walls dismantled, Buckingham Palace was never located.'"

Simon wished Ike would stop reading aloud and go home. "Maybe it was just a story the guards made up to scare the prisoners."

"Yeah, maybe. And later the boys."

"Boys?" Ammy jerked her head up. "What boys?"

"The ones in the school," Ike said. "Remember Mr. Manning said there was a school? Where Harry Ralston's grandfather worked? Well, after the jail closed, the building stayed empty until 1920. And then the Society for the Reform of Wayward Youth bought it." He flipped pages. "Here we are. They called it the Dunstone Training School, but the book says it was 'little better than a prison for children.'"

"Ike," Ammy said.

"'It was reported later that the practice of confining inmates in Buckingham Palace was continued, unofficially, in the school,'" Ike read.

"Ike!" Simon said.

"'The headmaster's regime ended in an official hearing into charges of abuse, and the school was closed in 1931. The school directors were convicted of—'"

Ammy reached over and yanked the book out of Ike's hands.

"Hey!"

She clapped the book shut and shoved it under Simon's pillow. "Go home, Ike. Sweet dreams!"

After Ike went home and Ammy went to her own room, stretching and rubbing her eyes, Simon moved the books to his desk. The history book slid off the one below and fell open to the chapter Ike had been reading. He reached to close it, but something caught his eye. A face looked up at him out of a grainy blown-up photograph.

It was a boy's face. A young face with too-big eyes and thin cheeks. The eyes seemed to be looking at Simon and asking him something. Asking what?

He closed the book and went to brush his teeth, still thinking about that face. He felt guilty about shutting it up like that without even finding out who it was. That's silly, he told himself in the mirror. But when he came back to his room he opened the book again and read the caption under the photo.

Jacob Redding, age 14, sent to the school for vagrancy ... poor family ... depths of the Great Depression ... begging on the streets of Toronto ... unaccounted for when the school was closed and the boys dispersed ... ran away, the headmaster said, but ... never traced.

That was all there was about Jacob Redding. But the eyes still looked out of the page, still asked a question. Maybe it was "Why?" Simon thought. Taken from his family and locked up, just because he begged on the street! How was that fair?

Simon closed the book. He wished he'd never seen that photo. He almost wished he was small enough to go and ask Celeste for a hug.

WHEN AMELIA got to her room she was so tired she could hardly find her backpack beside the door where she'd flung it, let alone dig out her favourite pyjamas. They were actually a pair of footless black tights and an oversized black T-shirt with a roaring tiger graphic on it.

Her eyelids shut down by themselves as soon as her head hit the pillow. Ty, she thought, and the image of him came to her — not the lost boy with pigeon feathers stuck to his face, but Ty as she'd last seen him on Mythrin: a warrior of the Urdar. *Ty! Ty, where are you?*

Sleep wrapped her up and carried her away.

SHE FELT as if she'd been searching forever. Climbing, nosing into this cave and that cranny, and then climbing on. Now she was near the top. She squeezed into a narrow canyon that led upward in a staircase of many steps, up and up around the mountain's spire.

One last push, and she was standing on the spire's flat top. A cold wind tore at her hair and flattened her thin clothes against her body.

Too cold. This human body was so weak!

Then change it.

And quick as that, talons sprouted from her fingertips. Shining red-brown scales spread from her hands up her arms. Wings unfolded from behind her shoulder blades and spread wide. She turned her long neck and gazed with satisfaction back along the length of her powerful body and long, barbed tail.

She sprang forward, gripped the edge of the cliff-top, and gazed. Far below spread the gold-glinting land. Far above shone the starry ocean of the sky. *Fly!* the stars called. *Fly!*

She crouched like a spring pressing down. Out swept the great wings, and she leaped into the abyss.

Behind her, somebody shouted *Ammy! No!*

AMELIA WOKE. She'd been dreaming. Now she was falling. King Street whirled up at her, a blur of lights between her out-flung human hands.

Chapter 10

Ammy in the Sky

THE OLD WINDOW frames in the Hammer Block leaked cold air in winter. Simon pulled the quilt up to his chin. He floated between sleep and waking.

In the waking moments he kept seeing Jacob Redding's face. He wondered where Jacob had slept. Did he have a warm bed like this? Had anybody checked on him in the night to make sure he hadn't kicked the covers off, the way Celeste still did sometimes, when she thought Simon was asleep? He didn't think so.

In the moments of sleep he saw rough stone walls closing in on all sides, crushing him into the centre of a tiny patch of floor. He woke to find himself curled up into a shivering ball.

Buckingham Palace, Simon thought as he drifted off again. Had Jacob ever been shut up there, in the cold and the dark and the silence?

It had to be just a story. Who would ever do a thing like that to a kid?

Never traced ... what happened to ...

Half asleep and half awake, he heard footsteps, slow and soft, pass his door. It wasn't Celeste, who had a firmer tread. It had to be Ammy.

Ten minutes later, a question jarred him awake. The footsteps had not returned. Ammy hadn't gone back to bed. The display on his clock radio said eleven forty-four.

He got up and tiptoed along the corridor, careful not to wake Celeste, who always slept with one ear tuned, like radar. Ammy's bedroom door was halfway open. The baseboard light in the hall reached in and showed her bed rumpled and empty.

Next stop, the front door of the apartment. Celeste locked up and shot the dead bolt every night, but now the bolt was open. Simon shook his head at it, then went back to his room and pulled on warm socks and slippers, and a fleece dressing gown over his pyjamas. He slipped a small flashlight and his bunch of keys into the dressing gown pocket.

He let himself out into the corridor and softly closed the apartment door. Then quick down the stairs to the King Street door. The locks hadn't been touched. So Ammy hadn't gone outside. At least, not this way.

He didn't bother checking the basement or the security door at the back. If Ammy was sleepwalking, like she'd been doing that time last winter (for the first and only time in her life, she'd sworn), she'd be heading upward. Especially if a dragon dream had anything to do with it.

When he pushed open the door to the roof, a blast of wind took his breath away. The door slammed behind him. He looked around. No Ammy. Maybe, after all …

Oh no.

There she was. Standing on the parapet looking down on King Street. Her bare toes curled over the edge.

"Ammy," he said softly, and walked towards her. *Careful, don't scare her!*

She shook back her hair. Then she crouched, her arms swept wide, her head rose, and — "Ammy! No!" — she jumped.

For one moment, while Simon's heart seemed to stop beating, Ammy hung there in mid-air. As if she really might fly.

67

And then she dropped. Someone screamed.

THE SCREAM ROSE as Amelia fell. It cut off when a pair of new-formed wings cupped the air. The sudden mid-air stop drove the wind from her lungs. Her newly clawed feet scrabbled across something smooth and hard.

And then, with a single downward beat, she surged upward again. Streetlights and lit windows flashed past. A face gaped at her from a rooftop — Simon! He waved both arms over his head and shouted something she couldn't hear.

One more wing-beat, and Simon and the rooftop dropped. Instinct told her to get higher, to find the safe darkness above the electric glare. She spiralled up and up until Dunstone was only a sprinkle of lights far below. A faint haze, or buzz — it was sound as much as light — lay over the town.

The wind whistled under her wings. She screamed again, this time from joy.

I did it! I changed! Here on Earth!

Only ... how did I do it?

Amelia kept circling, barely moving her wings. How had it happened? She'd been sleepwalking again. For only the second time in her life. And in her dream she'd been a dragon. She'd taken flight.

And then woke up, and it was only a dream, and she was human after all.

And then, of course, fell. And really did change shape, right in mid-air. Or maybe low-air, judging by the way her claws had scraped. *That was close! Wonder what I nearly hit?*

Panic had saved her. Flipped a switch inside, forced the change.

Now if only I could figure out how to flip the switch on purpose! I don't want to have to throw myself off a tall building every time. It might not always work.

Amelia rolled over and rowed the wind-stream with her wings. She gazed up at the stars. How they glittered! And what sharp colours! This felt so amazing! Like running at top speed after being cooped up at a desk all day. Like swimming in a warm sea. So easy, so right.

And ... she twisted her neck to get a look at her wings ... *I'm almost certain I've grown since last summer. Yes! I have! I'm bigger!*

She rolled over again and looked at the land below. The faint buzz, or hazy cloud, or whatever it was that lay over Dunstone was stronger now. Suddenly she knew what it was.

Thoughts! It was the thoughts of all the people in the town. Now that she'd grown a bit, she was getting better at doing dragon things, like...

Like tuning in on people's minds.

Ty! Why can't you help me figure this out? Why can't I reach your mind now?

She closed her eyes and listened hard. Nothing answered. She spiralled downward. The lights of Dunstone lined up and formed streets. The buzz of thoughts grew louder. Where in all that was Ty's voice?

She dared to swoop lower. Now she pictured the voices as glowing threads. They were mostly washed-out pink or watery blue or pale violet. Together they wove that greyish, buzzing cloud.

It shouldn't be hard to pick out Ty's thread. It wouldn't be like the others: it would be stronger and brighter. She circled lower, searching, listening.

As she flew above the Hammer Block, one of the pale voices separated from the cloud. It flashed a picture at her: Simon. He was yelling, but it only came to her in scraps. *Ammy... get ... watch ... Ammy!*

It's Amelia! she snapped, and laughed to feel how he jumped.

Words flashed back at her. *Ammy, get down! Change back! They've seen you!*

Who, she began, then waved Simon's voice out of her head. Ty's voice suddenly ran there, strong and bright as she'd known it would be, a thread of blue-green light.

She'd flown far out to the west, past the last lights of town. Now she flipped in mid-air and flew back, lower, skimming the rooftops, too excited to care who might see.

The closer she came, the surer she was where to find him. Just a hop and a step from the mall. The Queen Street bridge. Not on it, under it.

Ty! Ty, wait! I'm coming! I can help!

Chapter 11

Falling Star

SIMON WATCHED the big, winged shape fade upwards into the darkness beyond the reach of the streetlights. He exhaled a cloud of vapour and let his arms drop. This was a disaster!

So she'd finally done it. She'd figured out how to turn into a dragon here on Earth. Now there'd be no stopping her. And sooner or later — probably sooner, knowing Ammy — she'd get careless and somebody would see her and then — kapow! Open season on Amelia Hammer, teenage dragon.

He leaned over the parapet and looked down. Lucky she'd changed when she did, or she'd have bounced off the roof of that Volkswagen parked under the streetlight. It was Vern Sparks's old yellow VW Beetle, and there was Vern standing in the road with a cell phone in his hand. He was squinting upward. Now he was tapping a number into the phone.

Oh-oh. Vern's calling the police, I bet. What did he see?

Simon shoved his freezing hands deep in his pockets. He craned back his head and turned slowly around and around, searching the sky. There was no moon, but the cold, dry air was like polished glass. The stars shone diamond-bright.

He thought of all the things Ammy could run into at night, if she wasn't careful. Hydro pylons. The radio mast on Beacon Hill, to the west. Founder's Tower, up on the ridge. Weather balloons. Small aircraft. Large birds.

Ammy, where are you?

Another car stopped in the street below. Doors opened and slammed. Voices murmured. Simon looked over the parapet again. An OPP car stood behind the Volkswagen. Vern was talking to the two officers and patting the roof of his car. He waved his other hand upwards. They all started to look up. Simon quickly backed away from the edge.

Ammy, hurry up! He wondered if she could hear him. The other times she'd been in dragon form she could hear his thoughts without even trying. He'd always hated that. Hated the idea that there was no private place in his own mind, when Ammy-dragon was around.

Now he hoped she could tune him in loud and clear. *Ammy! Can you hear me?* It felt strange and clumsy to shape words in his head, instead of just thinking. He listened. No answer. He tried again. *Ammy, get down now! Only, watch out — don't come down on the Hammer Block!*

He listened. Still nothing. *Ammy!*

IT'S AMELIA!

The shout exploded in his mind. He jumped. Her laugh bounced painfully inside his head.

Ammy, get down! Change back! They've seen you!

Who—

And then she was there. A huge, silent shape that cleared the parapet on the west by eighteen inches, at most, and rose to skim over his head. A shadow against the stars, a gust of wind, the smell of burnt cloves. Then gone, leaving one joyous thought, not his own, to burn across his mind like a shooting star. *Ty! Wait!*

Somebody yelled on the street below. It was Vern. "There! There! What did I tell you?"

Simon leaped into the stairwell hut. Eastward, he thought as he rattled down the stairs. Eastward, in a big hurry. Not a thought in her

72

head except finding Ty.

One idiot with a shotgun. That's all it'll take.

THE BRIGHT THREAD of Ty's thought reeled Amelia straight towards the Queen Street bridge. Wallace Street flicked past below, then a blur of rooftops, then a gap — Bain Street. And then, dead ahead, the town hall tower. It swung at her like a giant baseball bat.

If she hadn't been flying like a speeding bullet, she could have swerved around it. If she hadn't sliced so low, she could have soared over top.

She almost made it. The tip of one wing cracked on one of the stone dragons carved around the edge of the parapet. Pain shocked through her wing to her shoulder.

Speed carried her over the mall on a long downward curve. The Dunn River lay ahead, a white serpent thrashing in its rocky prison. Down and down she coasted, and then she wasn't coasting: she was falling.

Amelia's strong talons pulled back into thin, weak, pale human fingers. Her wings beat feebly, and then not at all.

With a shriek, she dropped into the gorge. The current swallowed her. Then it spat her into the air, snatched her back, rolled her head over heels, poured water down her throat, and bounced her from rock to rock.

Then a sudden stop. A cedar stump that stuck out sideways into the river had caught her body like an outstretched arm. She clutched it and hung there gasping and coughing. The current sucked at her legs below the stump and wrenched at her shoulders.

Alive, she thought. But for how long? Her dragon strength was gone. Her hands and arms were numb. Her fingers slid on the slippery wood. The river roared hungrily.

She turned her head, and saw a face — no body, just a face —

73

looking down at her from the other side of the gorge, under the bridge. Reflected light gleamed off black-button eyes.

Help me! she screamed, or thought. Then her arms gave way, her hold slipped, and the river swallowed her.

THIS IS USELESS. I'll never find her. Why am I even trying? Simon stopped on Riverside Drive, east of the Queen Street bridge. There wasn't a sight or sound of a car.

The sky overhead was black and empty. Ammy could be halfway to Toronto by now, the speed she'd been going.

So, thanks to Ammy, here I am out on a freezing night in my dressing gown and slippers. Again. He muffled his hands in his sleeves, turned around and scuffed back towards the Queen Street bridge, where Queen crossed the river and King Street turned into Riverside Drive.

He was a few yards short of the bridge when he saw somebody running towards him along the top of the stone wall that kept people from falling into the gorge. The dark figure jumped down from the wall and landed lightly in front of him. "You!" it said. Simon backed off, then stopped and looked again.

It was Ty. He was a mess. The hoodie he'd got from Simon was frayed and filthy. Dirt or dried pigeon blood smudged his face. His eyes were two gold glints behind a curtain of hair.

"Ty? Are you, um, okay?"

The golden eyes blinked. "Okay-y?" He rolled the word around in his mouth, tasting it. "Yes," he said. "No." Then he jumped up on the wall and pointed across the gorge. "That one can't fly. It can't climb."

"Um, what one? Who?"

Ty hissed. He jumped down again, grabbed Simon by the wrist, and set off at a fast trot towards the bridge. Simon staggered after

74

him. "Hey!" he protested. "What? Stop!" He pulled back, but Ty just yanked him along faster.

When they reached the bridge, Ty swung Simon like a stone in a sling and let go. "She!" Ty called after him. Simon stumbled forward, windmilling his arms to keep from falling flat. When he caught his balance and stopped and looked back, Ty was gone.

She. She who? Simon looked along the bridge and saw a person-sized heap on the sidewalk. He sprinted.

Ammy was soaked, hair plastered to her head, thin black clothes stuck to her body. She looked like a half-drowned kitten. She looked up at him, white-faced, trembling. "T- t- t-," she said.

"Tell me about it later. Let's get you back before Celeste catches us." He took hold of her arm. It was icy and dark with bruises. "My gosh! Here." He pulled off his dry, warm dressing gown and poked her arms into it and sashed it around her.

Then he took off his slippers and socks and worked the heavy socks on over her limp, cold feet. The slippers would have been too big.

"Ow!" Ammy shook her right foot. "Splinter."

Simon took off the sock and squinted at her toes. "It's not a splinter. It's a chip of..." He pulled it from under her big toenail and held it up. Hard to tell in this light, but it looked a lot like... "Yellow paint," Simon said flatly. "Yellow Volkswagen paint."

"Volkswagen!" Ammy stared blankly. Then she giggled.

Simon sighed and tossed the chip over the bridge railing into the gorge. "No wonder Vern was so excited. I wonder what the roof of his car looks like."

By this time Ammy had the strength to stand up and limp along, wincing at every step. By the time they'd crossed the bridge, she could say more than one word at a time.

"So you fell in the river?" Simon said. "Lucky you didn't

drown!"

"I would've, if not for Ty! I was just about finished." She shuddered. Then laughed. "He was amazing! He pulled me out of the river and then he carried me up the side of the gorge."

"Pretty cool."

"Better than cool! You see what it means, right? Something inside him knows me! Now we just have to get him to stay put long enough so I can talk to him. Make him remember."

Vern and his Volkswagen were gone from beside the Hammer Block. The police were gone, too. Simon was beginning to hope that maybe, against all the odds, they'd come out of this mess without getting into deep doo-doo first.

They ghosted into the apartment. Simon soundlessly locked up. Then he heard Ammy: "Uh-oh." When he turned around, there was Celeste in her purple velour robe, standing in the kitchen doorway with her arms folded.

"Where on Earth have you been at this hour?"

"We were out looking for Ty." Ammy huddled deeper into Simon's dressing gown. "I fell in the gorge, and Ty pulled me out." She sniffled and coughed feebly.

"Fell in the gorge! Girl, you could have been killed! Simon, I thought you were the sensible one. Why didn't you stop her?"

While talking, Celeste was sweeping Ammy towards the bathroom, giving Simon no chance to explain that it would be easier to stop a charging bull moose than to stop Ammy from doing anything she wanted.

"Hot bath, then bed," Celeste said. "Tomorrow we'll all sit down together and have a quiet talk. This is the last time you two do any night-roaming."

Chapter 12

Danger – Do Not Enter

ON SUNDAY, after breakfast, Ammy and Simon and Celeste sat down together around the kitchen table and had a quiet talk over cups of hot, sweet, Indian-spiced tea.

It was about as gruesome as Simon had expected. Ammy survived it a lot better than he did, but that was nothing new.

She'd survived the night better than he had, too, which didn't seem fair, seeing that he'd spent most of it trying to save her butt. As they headed out to meet Ike, with Celeste's warnings ringing in their ears, Simon was still groggy from lack of sleep. Ammy strolled along with a bounce in her step, hands in her jeans pockets. Even her bruises were almost all faded.

"I don't know why you're so uppity," he grumbled. "Nothing has turned out right. And we still don't know how Ty came to Earth, or what changed him or took away his memory."

"Well, maybe we will, soon." She swaggered annoyingly. "I saw something last night in the gorge. Something important."

AMELIA REFUSED to say anything more until they met Ike, a few minutes later. The three of them leaned over the stone wall bordering the south side of the gorge, across from the mall.

"There!" She pointed. "D'you see it? That green patch, right up under the bridge?"

Ike had Simon's binoculars up to his eyes. "There's a bunch of ferns and grass and stuff on the cliff under there. Okay, so?"

"It's under that," Amelia said. They both looked blank. "Man, you two are slow! It's the secret way into the caves under the mall!"

She'd expected at least a little whooping and leaping about, but the guys just looked sceptical. Ike had the binoculars up again. "That grassy stuff doesn't look like it could hide anything bigger than a groundhog hole. You couldn't get through that."

"Well, Harry Ralston got through it. So I can too."

"Harry Ralston?" both boys echoed.

"That's how I knew there was a cave behind there. That's who I saw looking down at me last night. Just like a rat peeking out of its hole."

"Ralston the Ratman." Ike laughed.

"You saw his face," Simon said. "Doesn't mean his whole body could get through. Or mine or Ike's or even yours. Or Ty's."

"Only one way to find out, right? Go see."

Simon took the binoculars and found the spot. He scanned slowly down the cliff, then up again. Lowered the binoculars and shook his head. "You can't do it. Can't get to it."

She took the binoculars and studied the cliff face. "There's a ledge about ten feet over the river. That'll be easy." She scanned upward. "The cave mouth is over that sticking-out bit about twenty feet above the ledge."

"That sticking-out bit," Simon repeated. "Right. You'll never get past the overhang."

"Says you!" She pushed the binoculars back at him and set off briskly towards the bridge.

"You'd have to be a spider!" Simon scrambled to catch up. Ike started singing the theme from *Spiderman*.

Amelia walked faster, to keep ahead of them. Something she'd never tell Simon: she wasn't one hundred per cent sure she could

78

climb that cliff. A year ago she would have been absolutely sure she couldn't. But a lot had changed since last winter, when she'd shared Mara's dreams. She wasn't the same girl.

I can do things. Things I don't even know I can do, yet.

Besides, it really made her mad when Simon tried to big-brother her. She could hear him muttering behind her. "This is crazy! You'll kill yourself!"

Across the bridge and a couple of blocks eastward along Riverside Drive, a path crawled down the north side of the gorge. It led down to a flat, stony landing where people launched rubber tubes and kayaks in the summer.

The path was steep and narrow, with log steps built into the steeper places, and a steel-pipe railing to guard the outer edge. The gap in the stone wall at the top of the path was closed off with a locked steel gate. The gate was only waist-high. The sign on it said DANGER — DO NOT ENTER.

The three of them read the sign. "Well, there you are," Simon said, as if that settled it.

Amelia looked both ways along the street and across the gorge. Along this stretch of Riverside Drive, the houses gave way to steep hillsides covered with fir trees. Hardly a person in sight, only a car or two whizzing by at top speed. Nobody paying attention.

"Ike?" Amelia held out her hand. "Didn't you always used to carry a flashlight?"

"Still do. 'Cause you never know, you know." Ike unhooked a metallic purple finger-sized tube from his waistband and handed it over. She zipped it into a pocket of her short leather jacket.

"Now, just wait a sec," Simon began, but by the time he got to "sec," Amelia was over the gate and on her way down the path.

After one step she could see why they put a danger sign up above. This path would be tricky enough to get down in dry weather.

Right now it was drenched with spray and slippery with mud. She slid and skidded, and travelled part of the way on her rear end. But she kept her balance, and reached bottom only a little scraped and muddy.

Of course, "bottom" now wasn't the kayak landing, which was deep under foamy water. In fact, there wasn't any flat place to walk at all. She had to scramble over algae-covered rocks, climb over slippery boulders, and haul tangles of driftwood out of her way.

In one place she had to jump from rock to rock above the water. In another place she had to crawl under an overhang. In no time she was soaked and covered with grime from her toes to her elbows.

A year ago I would have hated this!

She still wasn't thrilled about the cold and the grime, but now something in her bones told her she could do it. She felt light and strong and fiery, built of sunlight and steel. *Dragon.*

Glancing up, she saw two heads above the stone wall. They were pacing her up on the sidewalk. Every minute or so, a face peered down at her. *Stop doing that!* Much more of that and people would notice.

She reached the bottom of the cliff under the bridge, studied the cliff face briefly, then started up. This part was easy, almost like climbing a ladder, plenty of jutting rocks and tough cedar roots to hold onto.

A few minutes later she pulled herself onto the ledge and stood up. And looked up again. And then for the first time began to doubt.

The hanging mat of greenery bristled high above her head. The cliff face below it looked like somebody had scooped it out with a giant spoon.

I'd have to climb practically upside-down to reach that!

From here she could look up behind the green curtain. The cave mouth was plain to see. Weirdly, it did look exactly like a mouth, a slice of darkness maybe five feet long between two jutting boulders. The coarse grasses and ferns hung over it like a great big walrus moustache.

Thinking of the cave as something that could suck her in and chew her up and swallow her made Amelia's stomach curl up.

Cool it! It's only rocks! Ty wouldn't wait a second, he'd be up there by now.

Yes, said a sensible, Simon-like voice from a place deep inside her, *but Ty's a real dragon. You're not.*

"I am!" she said aloud. "Last night I flew!"

But you don't know how you did it.

Amelia packed the voice away and slammed a lid on it. Then she studied the cliff face again. It wasn't as bad as it looked. It didn't start to curve outward until the last five or six feet. Some of the longer, thicker shrubby things hung down that far.

If she could grab a bunch of those. And if they were strong enough to take her weight…

But if they aren't? Don't be an idiot. Climb down and go back.

Shut up! Amelia closed her eyes and took a deep breath. *Sunlight and steel.*

Still with her eyes tight shut, she began to climb.

It was easier this way, seeing everything by touch. She pictured her dragon claws curving out long and strong, finding the crevices, sinking in like rock climbers' pitons. Up and up she went, slow but steady. Sunlight warmed her hands and glowed red through her eyelids.

Something feathery and green-smelling brushed her face. That meant there were pockets of earth in the seams between the rocks. Her dragon toes found them and gripped.

Inch by inch, up and up. The sunlight flickered. A bird chirruped close by and took off with a rustle of leaves. Nearly there.

81

She kept on climbing.

Then came the moment when she felt up and touched stone overhead. This was where the cliff hung outward: the chin below the cave mouth's underlip.

Amelia froze. *Can't go farther. Can't ...*

It's only a few more feet. She pictured the tough shrubby stems hanging behind her. *All I have to do ...*

She opened her eyes. Her fingertips, black with dirt, clung to a half-inch of crevice here and a pea-sized knob of stone there. No talons. Nothing to dig in and hold her weight. Her toes started slipping. She shut her eyes and opened her mouth to scream.

Grab! Now! snapped the sensible inner voice. Amelia pushed off with her toes, reached and grabbed. Gripped two fistfuls of something that felt like twine twisted with wires. Swung at arms' end over emptiness. *Up! Don't just hang there! Up!*

She clawed upward, hand over fist. Her knees slammed stone. She groped with her toes, found an edge, something to grab onto. Lunged. Hung on a smooth curve of stone that was slowly sliding her off. Reached, pulled. Upward and inward.

Made it.

Amelia lay flat, breathing hard, heart pounding, eyes still tight shut. When her heart slowed down to near normal she opened her eyes. She was lying on the edge of the cave mouth's underlip. One fist still clutched a bunch of stems. They ended in short roots with clods of earth stuck to them.

So that's what was holding me? Feeling dizzy, she tossed the stems into the gorge. Then rolled away from the brink.

Now, after all that, if the opening was too small ...

But it wasn't. Amelia had to flatten herself and squirm to get through the cleft, but after that it opened up. Not much, but enough to let her crawl on hands and knees.

She got Ike's flashlight out of her pocket and held it in her right hand as she crawled. The dancing light showed where the rocks jutted up to bruise her knees and down from above to crack her skull.

The flat passage tilted until she was pushing her way along between the walls, and finally bent upright. It was harder to travel here, because the cleft narrowed down to a crack that kept trapping her feet.

Always the passage led downward. Amelia began to wonder whether it really did lead under the mall, or whether it would just get narrower and narrower and finally close up. And if she'd be able to turn around then, or if she'd be stuck there.

Just as she was wondering this, she came to a place where the rocky wall bulged out from the right side and curved in on the left. It left a C-shaped opening that a thin person might be able to squeeze through, if they could bend themselves around the bulge.

And then what? Did it get better or worse after that? Amelia shone the flashlight through the gap. The beam didn't show anything. It seemed to vanish into emptiness.

Emptiness. A cave? Holding the flashlight in her left hand, and turning sideways, she pushed her left leg through the lower part of the gap. Then bent forward from the waist and shoved her left arm and shoulder through.

Halfway through, she stuck. An arm and a leg scrabbled on each side of the C-shape. Her breath came short.

Don't panic! The sensible inner voice seemed to have taken charge, now that she'd got herself into this fix. *Make yourself small!*

Small. Okay. Amelia exhaled hard, pulling her stomach towards her spine. She pushed sideways. And then, with a stagger, she was through.

Chapter 13

Hunter in the Dark

"WHAT A PLACE!" Amelia murmured. The flashlight beam swung back and forth, lighting up the rough ceiling a few inches above her head and the rocky walls brushing her elbows.

It was not what she'd expected. She'd pictured a big, high cavern, its roof hung with limestone icicles. Maybe crystals glittering in the walls. Maybe veins of gold.

This was nothing like that. She stood in a stone passage just wide and high enough to move around in. Everywhere you looked, new passages opened. But none of them led anywhere. They all ended in blank walls.

Amelia's heart still pounded. She still felt closed-in and trapped. *Huh. Never thought I had that ... what's it, claustrophobia?*

But no mistake, this had to be the cave under the mall. Under the place where the prison used to be, and the so-called training school for boys. Tools had smoothed the floors and, in places, the walls and ceilings: you could see the marks. And many of the side passages had been closed off with roughly mortared bricks or stones.

She walked on, following the main passage. Nowhere did she see anything that looked like a world gate. Of course, that didn't mean anything. A world gate could look like nothing at all until the right touch woke it up. It could be any boring stretch of wall.

There seemed to be no other way out — out to the gorge, that is — except for the C-shaped gap. Why had they closed off the other passages?

She realized then, and stopped short. Now she knew why she felt so trapped.

Of course they'd been closed off. If you were running a prison, you wouldn't want prisoners finding their way down here and escaping. They hadn't bothered with the C-shaped gap, because they'd thought nobody could get through there. And they'd been almost right.

It was getting hard to make her lungs work. She felt light-headed.

Imagine some poor guy coming down here and thinking he'd got free, and running from passage to passage, always coming up against stone or brick. Her heart thudded, paused, thudded again. She sank into a crouch. The flashlight beam wavered over the floor, showing the marks of feet in the fine sand.

Feet? Amelia looked harder at the floor. These weren't her footprints. They ran ahead, where she hadn't yet walked.

Not just one kind of foot. Some were bare — you could see the marks of toes — and big. About the size of Simon's feet, she thought. Or Ty's! She shot up and bumped her head on the ceiling. "Ow!"

Yes! Of course! Ty had been here. He'd found his way up into the mall from here.

The other prints were from shoes. They looked like men's shoes, the leather kind, not sneakers. But they weren't much bigger than her own footprints.

These prints, one kind or the other, were going to show her the way up into the mall. Maybe she could get out that way, and not have to struggle back through the passage and climb down the cliff, which she wasn't sure she could do without falling into the river.

Wouldn't it be cool to sneak up behind Simon and Ike from behind as they peered into the gorge and tap them on the shoulder! Wouldn't they jump! She giggled.

Amelia kept the flashlight beam low and followed the trail. The passage widened out, the roof rose, and suddenly it turned a corner and became a corridor with walls of mortared stone blocks. The corridor was short and ended in a wall, with a rust-red iron ladder that climbed up into a crevice.

This must be it! The way up to the mall!

She took a step towards the ladder, and stopped. From above came the click of a door closing. Then the clang of feet on metal. Someone was coming down!

She tiptoed back, slipped into one of the deeper side passages, and switched off the flashlight. She held her breath and listened hard, with eyes closed tight.

Something pattered past the end of the passage. It sounded like an animal, something large and quick. A dog, maybe.

They're hunting me with dogs? The thought made her go cold, though she wasn't sure who *they* were. But she could guess. Easy to picture the mall cops clumping around with ferocious guard dogs tugging at leashes. Maybe there were alarm sensors down here.

But how would a dog get down that ladder?

Amelia opened her eyes. She was surprised to find that she could see. Not very well, but well enough to tell where the walls were. Dragon eyes, she thought. Good at seeing in the dark. That made her feel stronger and safer.

Just as she was thinking that, the pattering sound came again. Something ran past the end of the passage in the other direction. Something man-sized, but it had to be an animal, the way it ran: quick, fierce, hunched over as if to sniff out a trail.

Oh horror! What was that? Is it gone?

No. It ran back. It stood in the mouth of the passage, snuffling, working its nose above bristly whiskers. It wore a neat, dark suit and smallish leather shoes.

"What are you doing here?" it squeaked.

Amelia backed away. "M- M- Mr. Ralston?"

"You were in the mall yesterday! Causing trouble!"

"We weren't actually—"

"Now you're trespassing!" He scurried forward a few steps. "Snooping!"

"No!" She backed away again and came up against a brick wall.

"You can't get out!" He bared two long front teeth. "Girls like you should be locked up!" He beckoned with one sharp-nailed forefinger. "Come here!"

"No way!" Amelia got a good grip on the flashlight. *Where are my dragon skills now?*

"I said, Come here!"

He scurried at her, hands out to clutch, teeth bared. She shrieked and poked him in the eye with the flashlight. He clapped hands to his face. Amelia made a dash, elbowed past him into the main passage, and raced.

Feet scampered behind her. She grabbed a corner to swing herself around, glanced back, and saw him leaping after her.

There! There was the C-shaped crack. She jammed herself through it. And stuck halfway through, just like before. Breathed out, tried to make herself small. Hands with sharp nails clamped onto her wrist. She shrieked again and tried to flail her arm. Kicked her left leg.

None of that helped. He was pulling her back. He had hold of her arm now, his nails sunk into her leather sleeve.

The jacket, said her sensible inner voice. *That's why you're stuck. Get out of it!*

But it's my favourite! she wailed silently. At the same moment she was ripping at the zipper, wriggling out of the sleeves. The jacket slithered left and Amelia slid right. She pried her feet out of the crack at the bottom of the passage and struggled onward, outward.

Now he'll come after me! He's small enough!

But he didn't. Only his squeaky laughter followed her as she crawled towards the clean scent of the river. And his triumphant squeal: "You're in for it, girl! I have evidence!"

"SO WHEN I got out again, I slid over that rock lip and hung on the stems and dropped to the ledge. That wasn't so bad, though I wish I'd had a rope. Then it was just an easy climb down to the bottom."

"You took a lot of crazy chances," Simon said. They were meandering along King Street. Ammy was rubbing her arms and shivering. He had offered his warm navy blue jacket, but — typical Ammy — she'd refused. ("I'd look like a dork in that!")

"And you didn't find a gate," Ike said. "You didn't really find out anything new."

"I did so! I found out for sure there *are* caves under the mall. A gate *could* be there. And I found out how to get from the caves up to the mall. And I proved Ty was down there before. And Harry Ralston. And you know what I just realized?" She pulled them both to a stop in front of the town hall square. "That ratty little man didn't have a light. He could see in the dark just as well as I could!"

"Well, rats can do that," Ike said.

"He's not a rat," Simon said. "He's just a man who looks like a rat."

"And runs like a rat." Ammy shivered. "And sounds like a rat. You don't know how horrible it was. And he's got my favourite jacket!"

"That bothers me, what he said about evidence." Simon said. "What's he planning?"

They found out when they reached the Hammer Block. Celeste was waiting for them in the lobby with the two OPP constables and

Harry Ralston. Harry was clutching Ammy's leather jacket to his chest. As soon as Simon, Ike and Ammy filed in through the front door, Harry pointed a trembling forefinger and glared at them out of a swollen eye. "There she is!"

It could have turned out much worse, Simon told Ike later. Harry could have laid charges of trespass and assault. It helped that Ammy stuck by an almost completely true story, that she'd been looking for her friend Ty, didn't know she was trespassing, and only hit Harry in self-defence. "I thought he was going to bite me!" she said.

"Bite?" Lisa Nader frowned at Harry.

"Caves under the mall, eh?" Bob LeBrun whistled. "Wait 'til the mayor hears!"

Harry froze for two seconds. "No!" he squealed. "The girl's lying! There are no caves!"

"Then where was she trespassing?" Lisa asked.

Harry snarled, showing his teeth and looking amazingly ratlike.

Lisa Nader and Bob Lebrun took Harry outside for a private talk. Celeste sat beside Ammy on the stairs and put an arm around her.

"Are you all right, honey?" Celeste asked. "Did that man hurt you?"

"No, I'm okay," Ammy said. "Just a little shook up."

"Good," Celeste said. "You need shaking up."

Uh-oh, Simon thought.

When the police and Harry came back inside, Lisa Nader was carrying Ammy's jacket. Harry said he'd decided not to press charges. "Only because it would not be in the mall's best interests." He pointed at Ammy again, and his little black eyes glittered. "But you, Miss, are banned from the mall! Fair warning!" He whirled around and barged out the front door.

Lisa Nader looked, unsmiling, at Ammy. "You are really, really lucky."

"Oh, I know." Ammy made a face. "That guy—"

"I don't mean Harry Ralston. I mean you were lucky in the gorge. And in the cave, or whatever that was. Don't you know how dangerous that caper was? Suppose you'd got stuck in there? Suppose you'd fallen into some hole? What did you — and you and you—" Lisa Nader stabbed Ike and Simon with her eyes. "*What* did you think you were doing?"

"I told you!" Ammy crossed her arms. "Trying to find Ty. He's my friend! Am I gonna get my jacket back?"

Lisa tossed it over. "We've had this talk before. I think this had better be the last time. Before something serious happens."

"Oh, don't you worry," Celeste said, much too quietly. "Miss Amelia won't be doing any more snooping or spelunking. She's going straight home to her parents. And she won't be back in Dunstone until she's learned to act her age."

Chapter 14

On the Roof

IKE PHONED Simon an hour later. "Yeah, grounded," Ike said. "Celeste called my dad and ratted me out. I can't go anywhere until school tomorrow."

"And I can't come over? Why not?"

"My dad says we're a dangerous mixture."

"Us! When it's all Ammy's fault? Well, I'll be stuck here all day anyway. No, not grounded, but I might as well be."

Simon hung up and looked gloomily around the kitchen. "All the windows in the apartment," Celeste had said. "Every single one. And I don't want to see any streaks."

"DON'T TELL ME nothing's going on!" Celeste slapped the steering wheel with the flat of her hand. "I know about that business yesterday in the Lutheran bell tower. And last night's escapade in the gorge — that could have been the end of you! Your parents will have my hide. And now this! You're lucky Harry didn't try to make those charges stick!"

"Well, he didn't. Gran, please! I have to stay here and look for Ty. Please!"

"And let you miss school? Not likely!"

Amelia slumped deeper in her seat.

Celeste darted a piercing glance at her. "I can't believe this is just about that boy."

"Ty. He's got a name. Ty."

"You only knew him for, what? one day? two days? last summer. How can he be a friend?"

Amelia growled silently. Another fifty miles rolled by in steaming silence.

"Well," Celeste said in a bright new voice. "So, tell me. How's the new school?"

"It's all right." *It's brutal.*

"Have you made friends?"

"Oh, sure. Lots."

"Who are they? Tell me about them."

"Oh, *Gran!*"

"HEY, AMMY-SPAMMY, got your homework done?"

Amelia closed the fridge door and gave her father a long-suffering look. "Not all of it."

"Your mom got jam-jams from that nice bakery on Queen Street. When you're finished your homework, come down and we'll devour them."

"Like you have to bribe me with cookies! I'm not three years old!"

Clear as day what this was all about, of course. Her mother and grandmother were already sitting on the living room sofa with their heads together. They wanted her out of the way so they could get seriously into picking apart her behaviour, school performance, and friendships (or lack of), and lay plans to straighten her out.

Carrying a can of cola, Amelia climbed the narrow back staircase to her attic room.

She hauled her backpack out of a corner, sprawled on the bed, and dug out her math notebook. Something was scrawled in there. "Do pg 20-22." Dug in her pack again for *Foundations of*

Mathematics. Pages 20-22 were jam-packed with problems. She worked through them briskly and dumped the book on the floor.

What else was left over from Friday? Geography. What a gigantic bore. And her geography notebook didn't have anything written in it for that day, so how was she supposed to know what homework to do?

She drew a map: mountains in a row of many zigzags, a deep valley, a river, low hills, plains, an ocean shore.... Mythrin. Or at least, the small part of it that she knew.

Amelia tossed aside her geography notebook and pulled over the one for language arts. Here was a page dated for Friday. She'd written something at the top. "Beowulf." Then a row of monster faces with sharp teeth and horns. That would be Grendel. The word "monster," traced over several times with a black pen, so it sank into the page. And then farther down, in a space to itself, the word "alone," with lines beaming from it all around, to show what a bright and shiny thought it was.

Alone, like Grendel. And me. And Ty. Monsters all.

Didn't Petra say there was an essay we had to do? Amelia closed her eyes and tried to remember what Mr. DeSouza had been saying just before class ended. Nothing. Complete blank.

She wasn't getting anything done, lying around here. Might as well go up on the roof.

Things were always better up on the roof. It was as if the breeze up there blew through her brain and cleared out all the confusing gunk. She went to the window, pushed up the sash, and lifted out the screen. Then sat on the sill and swung her legs out onto the tiny balcony, which was barely big enough for her own two feet.

From here she could get up to the roof, using a chain-and-bar fire-escape ladder she'd bought at Canadian Tire. She'd had to do some fancy work the first time with a rope to get the ladder chained to the chimney, but after that, getting up was easy.

She climbed up the ladder to the eaves, then over a slant of shingles to the chimney. Then, holding onto the chimney, she stepped up onto a small, flat, shingle-covered space on the very top of the roof between the four chimneys. There was room up here for maybe two people, or three if they all stood and hugged each other.

Amelia sat down and crossed her legs. This was her eyrie. Dragons had eyries. This was hers, her high place, where she could gaze out over her territory and watch for enemies.

You could see for miles and miles. To the west was the CN Tower and the other towers of the downtown. North and east there were ordinary house roofs sticking up among red and yellow trees. Beyond them, more towers.

South, downhill, past more treetops and rooftops, you could see Lake Ontario. Beyond the curve of Ashbridges Bay you could see all the way to the pale blue line of the horizon, where sometimes there were long, low ships.

Today the lake looked hard as steel and cold as death. There were no ships, not even sailboats.

"Hey!" called a distant voice. Amelia searched down and around and spotted somebody waving from the sidewalk. It was Petra Nowak. "Can I come up?" Petra yelled.

Amelia hesitated, then waved. "Come up to my room and out the window. Just don't mention the roof to my parents!" she called down.

A few minutes later there was a scrabbling sound on the balcony, then a jingle of chain. Petra's sleek blond head appeared over the edge of the roof. She frowned up at Amelia, then climbed all the way up and sat down beside her between the chimneys.

She didn't seem amazed to find Amelia up there. She acted as if this was normal. Amelia felt a little let down.

"I'm sorry," Petra said grimly.

"For what?"

"Oh, for being snarky the other day. Saying you have no friends. You probably do have some."

"Yeah, I do." *In another universe.*

"So, like, if you need anything ..."

Amelia studied the view. *Go for it. See what happens.* "I could use some help with school stuff. I mean, if I could see your notes from Friday. Not to copy. Just to see what the assignments are."

Petra shrugged one shoulder. "No prob."

Amelia finally looked at her. "Why are you doing this?"

"Dunno. No, maybe I do. I look at you and I see me, a year ago. My parents split up and my mom dragged me here from Winnipeg. Lost all my friends. Everything I knew."

"Split up? That's shitty."

"Yeah, me and my brother, they divvied us up between them like the dishes and the furniture. I hated my parents. I hated Toronto. I hated everything and everybody. And then I started a new school and couldn't figure out why nobody wanted to talk to me. I figured they were just all snotty Toronto kids."

"You're doing okay now, looks like."

"I didn't work it out by myself. Another girl told me I was scaring everybody off. After a while I figured out I didn't want to be alone any more." She poked Amelia on the knee. "You could try smiling once or twice."

"What difference would it make? I'd still be alone. I'm not like other people." That sounded really snotty, and whiny, too. Amelia wished she could suck the words back out of the air, but it was too late.

"Alone? That's how I felt," Petra said. "I felt like the last Siberian tiger. You know, one of those species that's going extinct."

"But you weren't really. I—" She shut her mouth before more

stupid words could get out.

"Don't tell me. You're actually an alien girl from another world. Googly-eyed monsters blew it up and you came here in a space capsule, all by yourself. Right?" Petra sounded flatly serious but when Amelia snuck another glance at her, something was glinting in her eyes.

"Close." *If only I could tell her.*

They sat silent for a couple of minutes. Then Petra said, "Gotta go." She climbed back down the ladder without another look.

Amelia didn't expect to see her again, except in passing, in the school corridor. And who'd blame her? *She knows I'm holding back.*

She climbed back down to her room. Twenty minutes later, her father yelled up the back staircase. "Ammy! Package for you!" She went down and he was holding a big manila envelope with her name printed on it and six notebooks inside.

So Petra kept her promises. That was something.

Amelia spent the rest of the day doing homework, with breaks to share jam-jams with her parents and grandmother. "I'm beating my brains out over this essay," she announced with gloomy pride. It was true, too. Her essay was about Grendel and Beowulf and how they were different and alike.

Her parents looked puzzled, but relieved. Celeste looked as if she didn't believe her ears.

Chapter 15

Chasing the Ratman

AT SIX-THIRTY that evening, Simon stood on a chair in Celeste's bedroom and polished the last streak off the last window in the apartment. He was looking down at King Street just as the streetlights came on.

He had a good view of the flat roofs of the lower buildings across the street. He had an especially good view of Ty creeping along the roof of a store, peering over the brick parapet. Ty seemed to be pacing someone on the street below.

Simon tracked his gaze down. A man stood below where Ty was crouching. It was Ralston the Ratman. Why would Ty be interested in him?

Harry Ralston had stopped to look into the store window. MILITARY BOOKS & MODELS, said the sign. As he stood there staring in, Ty hopped up on the parapet.

If he jumps he'll kill himself! Simon thought. Or he'll kill Harry. Or both.

He slid the window up and pulled out the screen and stuck his head out. All that took him only a few seconds, but now Ty was leaning out. One more second and he'd be in the air.

"No!" Simon yelled. "Stop! Get away!"

Harry Ralston looked around, then up at Simon's window. Simon made get-away motions with his hands. Ralston stared and frowned but didn't move.

Ty leaped into the air, silent as a pouncing cougar. He dropped two storeys. Next moment there was a mixed-up rolling heap on the pavement.

Simon jumped down from the chair, burst out of the room and out of the apartment and down the stairs, and ten seconds later he was on the street.

The rolling heap on the opposite sidewalk broke apart. The Ratman squirmed out from under on all fours, then leaped up and sprinted. He made good time, too. Ty flipped to his feet like an acrobat and raced after him. Simon gallopped after Ty.

"Ty, stop!" he gasped. "Stop! You'll — only — get — in trouble!"

They ran in a spaced-out string east on King. They raced across Bain Street, they flew past the deserted town hall square. Ty put on an extra burst of speed. He stretched out an arm, he nearly had a hand on the Ratman's collar, and then —

A word boomed like summer thunder. Someone strode across the street. Ty stopped so short, he did a back flip and landed smack on his feet. John Lilac set a hand on his arm. Ty stared at him.

"I'll tell the police!" Harry squeaked. "You just wait!" He scurried off as Simon came thudding up.

Ty must have been living hard since yesterday. One sleeve of the hoodie was nearly torn off at the shoulder. His left knee showed through a rip in the jeans. Everything, even the red DAWG shirt, was grey with mud and dust. A piece of dead leaf stuck out of his hair over his left ear.

Ty pulled free of Lilac's grip. He pointed after the Ratman. "That one is an enemy! I know it in my bones! Why did you stop me?"

"To stop you destroying yourself, fool." Lilac tilted his head. "He spoke of police. Trouble. Come!" He looked at Simon. "You too."

Lilac grabbed one of Ty's arms and hustled him across the street

98

and around the back of the bookstore. Simon jogged behind. He would have helped, only it was plain that Lilac didn't need any help.

A laneway and fence ran behind the houses here, separating them from the trail that followed the gorge. Lilac shoved Ty through the back door into the bookstore, towed him up a narrow back staircase, and pushed him into a room on the second floor.

"Shut the door," Lilac said, and Simon obeyed. This was a man who was used to being in charge.

Ty turned in a circle on his bare heel. He stared wide-eyed at the walls, which were covered with crammed bookshelves, floor to ceiling. Piles of books teetered in the corners. The only other thing in the room besides books was a blanket-wrapped mattress on the floor, and books were piled even there.

"Sit down!" Lilac pointed at the floor.

"No!" Ty gave himself a full-body shake. The tatters of his jeans and hoodie flew. "Not here! Too small! Too close!" He whipped around and flung himself at the door, only to stop short at the end of Lilac's arm. "Out!" he yowled.

"Out, then," said Lilac. "But not to the street. To the roof."

He waited until he saw Ty's head bob. Then he let him loose.

THAT WAS HOW Simon ended up on the roof of Dunn River Books one cold October night, watching Ty and Lilac size each other up.

Ty prowled around like a cat in a strange house, scouting out the street on one side and the gorge on the other side, and the narrow alley between this house and the next one. He climbed the two chimneys, he sniffed the flues. All the while he kept sneaking looks at Lilac, then pretending he hadn't.

John Lilac sat quietly on a white plastic chair and watched Ty. Simon sat in the other plastic chair. It was dark up here, beyond the

99

reach of the streetlights. The starlight showed the shapes of things, but not much more.

It struck Simon that the most he could see of Ty and Lilac was their eyes. Ty's glances were catlike glints of gold in the dark. Lilac's eyes were small, bright, amethyst windows.

Here I am, he thought, alone with two mixed-up aliens with powers I can't even guess at. Powers they don't understand themselves. Maybe I should get back down those stairs. Quick.

Curiosity kept him in the chair.

"What, um, what was that word you used?"

Lilac looked at him blankly.

"On the street, I mean. You used a word. A foreign word. To stop Ty."

Lilac stared, then shook his head. "It's 'scaped my mind."

Ty, who sat perched on the edge of the nearest chimney, suddenly pointed at Simon. "I saw you! You face! On a door."

"*Your* face," John Lilac rumbled. "But true enough, I too saw the like."

Simon sat forward. "You remember where?"

"On a door." Lilac leaned back and gazed up at the stars.

"What, um…."

"A door of iron. On it the likeness of a boy, climbing, reaching up to snatch a star from the sky."

The starry window. After a moment Simon remembered to breathe. "Wh- where?"

"Where?" Lilac's eyes winked off and on as he turned his head. "That's lost to me still. I remember only that behind the door lay a cramped and heartless cell. And outside it a maze of stone. And I remember the clue — the scent of water — that lead me out by secret and narrow ways. And then Vesper found me." His voice softened.

"You wrong!" Ty leaped from the chimney and landed in front of

Lilac. He sank down on the gravel-covered roof, folding his legs under him. "There was a door, yes. And him picture on it." He waved a hand at Simon. "Him climbing, reaching. And stars. And then noises. Feet!" He leaned forward. "I saw that enemy!" he hissed.

"Who? Harry?" Simon pulled in another breath. "That man you chased just now?"

"Yesss!" Ty bounced where he sat. "He run at me, he bite." Ty showed his teeth. "I bite back, better, harder. He run. I follow. Up…" Ty made his hands prance upward in the air.

"Up stairs?" Lilac growled. "You must learn the words, boy, else they will take you for a witling."

"Up stairs, yes. And then a shining place with strange smells and more enemy who try to fight me."

"Enemies," Lilac said sharply.

Ty laughed like a rusty gate. "They fight like, like childs. So I go away."

Simon closed his eyes. They were talking about the starry window. The one in the Hall of Gates on Mythrin. And now it was here in Dunstone, too.

Like it's following me.

He looked up to see John Lilac watching him. "It takes no mind-reader, lad, to see your mind is troubled."

Simon cleared his throat. "I think you found a gate." The two of them were staring at him now. "A, um, a special door. I think that's how you came here from another world."

"Another world!" Lilac echoed.

Simon nodded. "And that gate has my picture on it. And I don't know why."

"Perhaps someone is calling you," Lilac said. "Perhaps it wants something that only you can give." To himself he muttered, "Another world. That would explain…" Then he fixed his glowing eyes on

Simon's face. "To me this has the smell of a quest."

Voices and footsteps sounded in the staircase behind the door to the roof. One of the voices was Lisa Nader's. Ralston the Ratman must have gone to the police.

Ty sprang up and vanished over the rooftops, westward.

Someone knocked on the door. "Open up, please," said Lisa Nader. "Police."

"Anon!" Lilac stopped with his hand on the doorknob. He looked at Simon. "I almost wish that you could turn aside from this quest. There's glory in it, but peril, too. Much will end if you achieve it. I feel that in my bones."

"I don't know," Simon said. "I don't understand."

Lilac shrugged. "No matter. If it is a quest, it may not be refused."

Chapter 16

Dragon Scales

AMELIA WOKE UP on Monday morning with a headache. Things went downhill from there.

It started with Petra before first class. Amelia walked up to her and held out the manila envelope with the six notebooks, and was halfway through "Thank you" when Petra grabbed the envelope and rushed off. Like she was afraid she'd catch a disease.

All morning, the teachers muttered at Amelia. She couldn't understand a word they said. Not even Mrs. Bloomer, who taught the Healthy Living course and led the sports programs, and had a voice built up by years of shouting across soccer fields and hockey rinks.

Mrs. Bloomer paced back and forth in front of the class, whacking a pull-down diagram of a human body *(no skin, just bones and muscles, yuck)* with a wooden pointer. Amelia watched intently, or seemed to. From time to time she glanced at her hands and pictured red-brown scales surfacing from under the skin, spreading along the wrist, shining like new copper.

If I can focus really hard, and make that happen. I could practice. I could get control. Just the scales on the hand, first. Then the claws. Then the wings.

If she could get control of the change, she wouldn't have to throw herself off a building next time.

She kept trying, staring at her hands, picturing the scales coming out. They stayed the same, smooth and pinky-beige, human.

Between classes, packs of kids slunk through the dim corridors, giving her sidelong looks. Petra must have told everybody to shun her.

At noon Amelia went to her locker to dump her books. She stared into the open locker, thinking how bad things were. *My head hurts. My stomach hurts. Maybe I really do have a disease. Better go home.*

And then she thought: Mara wouldn't run home with her tail dragging, would she? You bet she wouldn't. Mara would look them in the eye and give them a big, bright dragon grin.

"Hey! Are you okay?"

She whirled around. A boy stood there smiling at her.

"You've been staring into your locker for like five minutes," he said. "What's so great in there?"

"You've been watching me for five minutes?"

"Well..."

"Five minutes? Don't you think that's creepy?"

He opened and closed his mouth. She smiled brightly. He backed away. She slammed the locker door and clicked the lock and marched away into the lunchtime crowd, which parted around her.

Now that she'd decided to be like Mara, her appetite came back. She bought a dish of fries with poutine and a can of cola. She had a table all to herself in the lunchroom, although the other tables were crowded. If anybody came near, she gave them a brilliant dragon smile and they backed right off.

All except Petra, who sat down beside her and plunked down a carton of milk. Then she unfolded the waxed paper from around a sandwich that looked as if she'd brought it from home. Whole wheat bread with lettuce and cheese sticking out the sides.

"Are you sure you want to sit here?" Amelia put on a look of polite concern. "This is the plague table, you know."

"Don't be such a pain in the ass." Petra bit into her sandwich and chewed.

Amelia scooped up poutine with her fingers. Petra made a disgusted noise. "You ever use a fork?"

"Poutine doesn't need a fork. So, how come you ran off this morning like I had the Black Death?"

"I go to math tutoring, first thing Mondays. I was already late."

"Math tutoring? Why?"

"Why d'you think? I suck at it."

Petra, bad at anything? Amelia stared in amazement. "Funny! I'm pretty good at math. I suck at everything else."

"You shouldn't. You're not dumb."

Amelia waved that away. She knew she wasn't dumb. "So why were kids giving me the evil eye this morning?" She looked around the lunchroom. People were watching her. She waggled poutine-covered fingers at them at them and they looked away.

"They weren't giving you the evil eye. They were looking at you weird because you were acting weird. You cracked this crazy grin whenever anybody tried to talk to you. You looked like you could bite."

"Talk to me? When? Nobody talks to me."

"Dougie Tam did. I heard. He's a friend of mine. He's nice." Petra finished her sandwich and brushed the crumbs into the waxed paper wrapper. She folded the wrapper into a neat square. "But you wouldn't notice. You never notice anything except yourself, right? Like, what goes on in class. I bet there's nothing in your notebooks from this morning. You really want to flunk?"

"Who ever flunks?"

"You might just find out."

Ammy pushed away her half-finished lunch. She didn't really want to find out what happened to kids who sank to the bottom of the class. For one thing, it would cause endless trouble with her parents,

105

who fully expected her to grow up to be a brilliant engineer or Nobel Prize-winning scientist, or at least able to earn a living. For another thing, it would be humiliating.

"Okay, yeah, you've got a point."

"Okay!" Petra swivelled on her chair and tossed her wrapper and milk carton at the garbage can by the window. They popped right in. She swivelled back. "So here's what you do. Right now. You go and see this morning's teachers. You say you're sorry for missing stuff. You ask them to tell you the assignments."

"They'll give me a hard time. Especially Ol' Boomer. And somebody's sure to ask what's wrong, and then I'll have to think what to say."

"Well, what *is* wrong?"

Amelia wanted to tell her. She wanted to say: I don't know what I am, and I'm not sure what I want to be, and I'm afraid to choose.

Suppose I do tell her? Petra's cool. She won't freak.

"Hey," Petra said. "What's that on your hand?"

"What?" Amelia lifted her wrist — and there they were. A patch of glistening reddish-brown scales. Another scale surfaced slowly at the edge of the patch as she watched. *Oh no.* She could just see herself changing to a dragon right here in the lunchroom. Petra bug-eyed with terror. Kids screaming and running. Police sirens starting up in the distance.

No! Not here! Not now!

"I…" Amelia looked Petra in the eye. She made up her mind. "Those are dragon scales. I'm part dragon." She studied the patch of scales. It didn't seem to be getting any bigger. She looked up again and saw the look in Petra's eyes. Icy disdain.

She thinks I'm blowing her off. She thinks there's something wrong and I'm lying about it.

"Ha! Gotcha!"

106

Petra rolled her eyes to the ceiling. "Lame!"

"It's a rash. I must be allergic to something in this poutine." She shrugged. "I'd rather have dragon scales than allergies."

"You and me both. With me it's peanuts. That's why I bring my own lunch." Petra nodded downward. "Look, it's fading."

Amelia brought her wrist close to her eyes. The scales faded into nothing. She hadn't turned into Godzilla in the lunchroom, thanks be to heaven.

"You really are weird, aren't you?" Petra said. But the icy look was gone from her eyes.

"'Fraid so." Amelia stood up. "I've just got time to go see Ol' Boomer and the others."

"Go get 'em, Hammer."

As Amelia walked out of the lunchroom, she had the feeling that things were changing. Kids weren't staring at her, or not in the same way. That would be thanks to Petra.

But her heart felt like a lump of cold potato stuck in her chest. Even if Petra is my friend, she thought, I can never, ever tell her the truth. I'll still be alone.

Well, not completely alone. There'd always be Simon.

Chapter 17

The Starry Shoes

SIMON RETURNED the borrowed books to Mr. Manning on Monday morning. Ike had soccer practice at noon. There was no chance to talk until after school.

Simon summed it up as they headed east along McNairn Avenue, heads bent against a wet, November-smelling wind. How he was sure that Ty and Lilac both came to Earth through a gate hidden under the mall. And how the marker for that gate was a door that was a copy of the starry window, only made of iron instead of stained glass.

"A copy?" Ike echoed. "Or else the window on Mythrin was the copy. Like, it was trying to get your attention."

"Don't say that!" Simon shuddered. "John Lilac says it has the, um, smell of a quest."

"A quest! That is so cool!" Ike quickened his step. "C'mon, let's go!"

"If you're thinking of trying to get through that crevice in the gorge—"

"No way. Even Ammy had trouble getting through there. You," Ike punched Simon on the chest, "would stick like a cork. No, I mean the mall."

"Oh, right. Ammy saw that ladder going up—"

"So we just have to find it. From the top side."

Once in the mall, Ike wanted to take the escalator to the lower level right away. "First the shoe store," Simon said. They started along the left-hand corridor. Then Simon saw a cluster of grey-hoodied kids marching towards them. They darted back and into the right-hand corridor before Kevin and the quints could spot them.

The place was gloomier than ever. Simon peered into the weaver's shop. She didn't look up, didn't smile. She kept her head down and kept weaving. Ike and Simon slipped past.

"She looks like a prisoner," Simon muttered.

"It's creepy, all right. Listen, something's different." Ike looked around. "The harp music's off."

There was nothing on the sound system. Without it, you could hear the hiss of ventilation, mechanical clicks and clunks from the ceiling, the clack of the loom. Their own footsteps were loud in the stillness.

There was something about the mall today that reminded Simon of those pictures of the old Dunstone Gaol. He felt as if hidden people were watching him. He wanted to press his back against the wall and slide towards the exit.

Ike kept looking over his shoulder. His freckles stood out on his white face.

Halfway along the corridor, a narrow hallway crossed through the core of the mall. It led to washrooms, and doors with signs on them: Staff Only, and Electrical. It also led through to the left-hand corridor where the few normal stores were. They walked along the hallway and peered around the corner and found the corridor deserted. Doogie's Shoes and the Wired Zone next to it were the only stores open.

Simon tiptoed swiftly across to Doogie's Shoes. He stopped in front of the window, not expecting to be there long. He'd always been able to move on again with a load off his shoulders.

This time he stood and stared.

There they were. They sat on a glass pedestal under a bright spotlight. Midnight-blue high-tops with golden stars on the ankles. The shoes from the starry window.

"Hey!" Ike stuck out a quivering finger.

The pedestal glittered. The golden stars gleamed in the brilliant light.

"Uhn," Simon said. *I'm doomed.*

Ike poked both fists in the air. "Just like in the starry window! Quick! Buy them! Why're you just standing there?"

Miss Dogood beamed from the doorway. "Aren't they fabulous? Come in! Try them on!"

"No, I, uh." Simon backed off. "I, I can't afford them."

She waved at a sales banner over her head. "Everything's forty per cent off!"

"I, I got to think. Can't …" He turned and ran towards the King Street exit.

"Wait!" Ike yelped. "It's like a prophecy! You can't fight prophecy! You've got to buy them! Or else it'll all go wrong!"

They ran around the curve in the corridor and came in sight of the escalators. And stopped short. Simon ducked back into the darkened doorway of a closed-down Laura Woods Chocolate Shop. Ike crowded in beside him.

"What are they doing?"

Simon inched his head out. There was more activity at the front of the mall right now than he'd seen in weeks, but it didn't look good. The mall cops and peer monitors were herding people out.

"There's that man that lives under the railway bridge," Simon said. The man, whose name was Otto, sometimes came into the mall to get warm. Security One and Security Two were pushing him out the front door. The final push sent him sprawling on the sidewalk.

Kevin and the quints clumped together and walked in a menacing way, mirrored sunglasses flashing, toward three boys with mohawk haircuts and chain-hung leathers.

"Isn't that Erwin Ogilvy? And Jeff Brown and Xenon Demesnos?" Ike said. "Hey! There's gonna be a fight!"

The fight fizzled out after some shouting and shoving. Erwin and Jeff and Xenon slouched out to the street. The guards and the peer monitors watched them go, then wheeled smartly and came marching back. Simon and Ike flattened themselves against the darkened glass. Simon closed his eyes and hoped.

The tramp of feet, one-two, one-two, echoed in the corridor. He peeked through his eyelashes. The guards marched past, then Kevin, then the quints. Their faces all looked the same, Simon realized. *Like they're wearing masks.*

He must have made a sound, because Kevin barked, "Intruder!"

That was their cue. They leaped out of the doorway and ran. Or started to. Ike was ahead. Simon took two steps before something caught his feet from behind. He crashed.

When he looked up, he was surrounded by grey shapes with bald heads and mirrored sunglasses. Like great big insects.

"You!" Security One stabbed a leather-gloved finger at him. "You're banned from the mall."

Ike pushed through the ring of insect faces. "We're not doing any harm!"

Simon started to stand up, but Security Two set a hand on the back of his neck and pushed him back down. Simon's knees hit the marble floor with a crack.

Ike went white as speckled paper. "That's assault!"

"You're banned, too." Security One clamped an enormous hand on Ike's shrimpy shoulder and dragged him towards the exit. Security Two followed with Simon in his grip.

"You can't do this!" Ike twisted and thrashed. "Wait'll the press gets hold of this! Wait 'til the law gets here!"

Security Two rumbled with laughter. "Kid, we *are* the law."

"You are not!" Ike bit the man's hand. Security One yowled like a big cat and gave him a shake that made his head flop back and forth.

Simon was just trying to stay on his feet. There was no use yelling and fighting. The best plan was to get out while they still had all their arms and legs.

When they were a few yards short of the doors, a ragged shape burst from the up escalator. It bounded across the floor, leaped high, and slammed both feet on Security One's back. He crashed to the floor. Ike spun away.

Ty sprang up and danced around the fallen guard. "You have no honour!" he shouted. "You fight boys, hah! Now you fight me!"

Chapter 18

Coming to a Boil

SECURITY ONE was on his feet again, growling like a dog. Security Two moved in. Ty danced away from the clutching hands, whirled, and raced towards the food court. The guards trampled after him. Kevin and the quints stampeded after them.

A moment later the sound of breaking glass came from that direction.

Ike and Simon followed cautiously. They stopped in the corridor just outside the food court and peered around the corner. Things had gone strangely quiet. Ty was sitting cross-legged on a wooden table, gnawing at a large salami. The butcher shop window was broken.

Security One and Two were creeping up on him from opposite sides of the pioneer garden's ruined stone walls. Each of them was holding a thick steel bar. The peer monitors were at their backs, three to each side.

"We should warn him," Ike murmured.

Simon caught Ty's gleeful look over the salami. "I think he knows."

The guards suddenly piled through the gaps in the ruin. Ty shot up as if there were wings on his feet. He swatted Security Two on the ear with the salami, dodged Security One's steel bar, and leaped to the top of the ruined wall. He danced there, waving the salami.

"You slow!" he shouted. "You worms!"

Movement on the mezzanine balcony caught Simon's eye. Harry

Ralston was leaning over the balcony railing. "Catch him!" he squealed. "Lock him up! He's a criminal!"

Ty looked up. He pointed the salami. "You! Enemy! I destroy you!" He tossed the salami over his shoulder and leaped again, up and out over twelve feet of air.

"He'll crash!" Simon gasped.

But next moment Ty caught the edge of the balcony floor in his hands and a half-second after that he was over the railing and leaping in pursuit of Harry Ralston, who was already halfway around the mezzanine towards the stairs.

Security One and Two charged up the stairs. The mall echoed with shouts of fury and shrieks of laughter.

Simon nudged Ike. "I don't like the way this feels."

Ike laughed. "Ty's playing with them! He's awesome!"

"He's playing. They're not. This is getting crazy."

Ike laughed again. He was getting a bit crazy too, Simon thought. There was craziness in the air. The mall felt like a big pot of soup coming to a boil. Any minute now it was going to bubble over.

"Ike! We've got to get out of here!"

"Not without Ty! He's the man!"

"We've got to get him out, too."

"Yeah?" Ike laughed. "How?"

Simon did the only thing he could think of. He walked out into the food court and shouted. "Ty! Come down! You've got to leave!"

He had to call two more times before Ty paid attention. He was standing on the mezzanine balcony railing, trying to knot Harry Ralston's striped tie around his head. He looked down. "This too fun! You go!"

"We can't go without you! And we'll get in trouble if we stay!"

"Then you fight!" Ty pranced on the railing, jabbing the air with his fists.

114

The Ratman, cowering in a corner of the mezzanine, watched Simon with glittering eyes. Three of the peer monitors were sneaking in this direction. Security One and Two were staring at him from the stairs and hefting their steel bars.

Simon's heart pounded. "Ty! I can't fight like you! Please come down!"

"Okay." Ty tossed Harry's tie aside. "Enough fun. I come." He leaped from the balcony railing to the stone wall to the wooden table to the floor and set off running without missing a step. Simon and Ike raced after him. Bellows of rage broke out behind them.

Ty was soon far ahead. They saw him leap high, twist in mid-air, and drop down the escalator well at the front of the mall. When they reached the spot they clattered down as fast as they could go. Ty was out of sight.

It was even darker and emptier down here than on the main level. It looked as if these stores had been closed for months. Their dusty glass fronts made Simon think of giant aquariums full of dark water. With big fish lurking in them just beyond the reach of the light.

Ike looked around. "There are the famous vending machines." Half a dozen of them stood against the base of the escalator. "I wonder if they're still vending centipedes."

Simon walked slowly around the curving corridor. It was getting darker and darker. "Well, at least it seems like they've given up chasing ... um ..."

Heavy feet crashed on the escalator.

Ike and Simon took off. A dozen strides carried them around the curve of the corridor. And then they stopped so short they piled up against each other.

Unlike the floor above, this corridor didn't loop around. It ended in a blank wall. They were trapped.

Chapter 19

Whose Bones?

SIMON SET his back against the blank end wall of the corridor. Ike lined up beside him.

"This is the worst," Ike began. Then he went "Wuh!" as the wall gave way behind him. The two of them fell backwards. They landed flat on their backs and lay there looking up. Ty stood blinking down at them in surprise.

Turning his head, Simon saw that what he'd thought was a wall was just a sheet of white-painted plywood. This part of the lower level was being renovated: that's why it was boarded off. He scrambled up and pulled the plywood back across the gap. Ike jumped up and helped.

"Quick!" Simon spun around. "Where can we hide?"

"Come!" Ty darted around the corner, past stacks of gyproc, dangling electrical fixtures, and pyramids of paint cans. Ike and Simon followed, just in time to see him flit through a door, which closed behind him.

The door was made of dented wooden planks. It looked as if it had been there longer than the mall. A sign was stencilled on it in black paint.

OFF LIMITS - POSITIVELY NO ENTRY

"That seems pretty clear," Ike said. He opened the door and they stepped inside. It was dark. Ike unhooked the purple mini-flashlight from his belt loop and shone it around.

They saw a room about twice the size of Simon's bedroom closet. Opposite the door was a rough stone wall. To the left were shelves holding jugs of cleaning fluid, tubes of glue, boxes of nails, rolls of duct tape, coils of copper wire, and dozens of other hardware-type things.

All that and no Ty.

"But he went in here!" Ike insisted. "We saw him!"

"I know. So that means..." Simon glanced over his shoulder. Voices growled in the corridor outside the plywood barrier. Wood scraped on concrete.

In two seconds Ike and Simon had the door closed and the flashlight off. They crouched down at the end farthest from the door. Hard things that smelled of oil and metal bumped against the back of Simon's head.

Heavy footsteps and gravelly voices sounded outside the door. The handle rattled. The door hinges creaked. Simon shut his eyes and crouched smaller.

Then another voice outside the door squeaked, "No! Leave that alone. Don't you see the sign? No entry! That applies to you, too!"

"But the lock's broken," Security One rumbled.

"Never mind. You leave it alone!"

The footsteps moved away. Simon waited until his heartbeat had settled back down to normal. Then he said, "You know what that means."

"Yeah. This is the Ratman's secret. So secret he won't even share it with the mall cops."

"His secret way down to the caves. And Ty found it, coming up the other way."

"So where is it, this secret entrance?"

Now that they knew it had to be there, it took them about one minute to find it. One section of the far left-hand wall, which looked like plain wood hung with tools on hooks, was actually a hinged door.

They pulled it open and stepped through, Ike first, with the flashlight. They crowded together in the dark on the edge of a crack in the bedrock. Ike shone his flashlight down into the crevice. "Looks like it goes down a ways. And guess what, there's a ladder. Just like Ammy said!"

Simon crouched down and found the top of the ladder, a rough metal bar fixed to side pieces that were bolted into the stone.

"Wow, this could've been here a hundred years!" Ike whispered.

"It probably goes back to the time of the prison. I think they just built the mall on the jail's foundation." Simon poked a thumb backward. "That lower level, if you cracked off the new plaster, I bet you'd find the old stones."

"Down we go." Ike turned around, knelt, slipped the flashlight strap around his wrist, and reached a foot down. The swaying beam made the crevice seem to open and close like a mouth.

When Ike's head disappeared, Simon started down. The rungs creaked and jerked away from the wall. He froze until the juddering stopped. "Not too solid," Ike called up. "Try not to put your full weight down."

"Yeah, big help!"

When they got to the bottom, Ike ran his light up the ladder. The bolts that held the side pieces to the wall wobbled in their sockets. Simon was wobbling too. "I could have broken my neck! It's only strong enough for the Ratman. Or you."

"Ty's big too."

"He probably just takes a giant leap and he's up. Or down."

"Never mind, we're here! In the secret caves! Let's explore!" Ike said in the shiny-bright voice he used only when he was really nervous.

They called for Ty, but he didn't answer. As they walked slowly through the maze of passages, Simon wished they had a couple of heavy-duty industrial flashlights instead of Ike's pencil-thin beam. For one thing, with a better light he wouldn't bump his head so much. For another, it was hard to really see anything with that flickering little ...

Flickering.

"You, um, you've got extra batteries, right?"

"Ah, no."

"Then let's hurry up and find the gate. I don't want to..." He didn't need to finish. *To be lost down here in the dark.*

The light rippled over rough stone walls and slid into side passages. Never anything to see but stone or mortared brick.

"We don't even know what to look for," Ike grumbled. "What did John Lilac say about the door?"

"Just that it was made of iron." A quest, Simon reminded himself. *Something I have to do.* All the same, he wouldn't be sorry if they never found—

"Hey! Look!"

The feeble light ran up and down the end of one of the side passages. Back behind a bend, almost out of sight, stood a dark slab.

"Give me the flash." Simon stepped forward and ran the beam around the outside of the door. It fit snugly. The surrounding stone looked as if it had been chipped and smoothed to match the shape of the door. The arched top was only a little higher than his head.

"This can't be it. There's no picture." He ran the light all over the door. Rough, rusty iron. Nothing at all like the starry window.

"Maybe the picture is on the inside." Ike pulled at the door. It swung outward easily.

"Funny," Simon said. "It opens real smooth. It should be all stiff and screechy."

"Bet this is part of the Ratman's big secret," Ike said. "He probably keeps these hinges oiled. Maybe he likes to sit in here and eat peanut butter and jam sandwiches."

Ike got the light back and swung it around. A cramped and heartless cell, John Lilac had said, and he was right. In fact, it wasn't even a cell, just a cave. Close to the door it was about six feet high and three feet wide. From there it sloped down until, at the back, it was just a slot in the stone.

"There's nothing in here at all," Ike said. The light ran over patches of grey moss and green-stained cracks. It stopped on a small pile of something in the back. "No, I'm wrong. There's a bunch of rags." He got down on hands and knees, reached in and poked the heap with a finger. The rags melted like cobwebs.

"Yi!" Ike jumped up, hit his head on the ceiling, and sat down hard. The flashlight flew up. Simon lunged and caught it. He focussed the light on the heap of … bones.

"It's a skeleton!" Ike yipped. "Let's get out of here!"

Simon knelt down beside the bones. After the first jolt, the skeleton wasn't scary or horrible at all. The bones were just brown and small and kind of sad. The skeleton was curled up, as if it was trying to keep warm.

Maybe like he was before he died. Simon's mind skittered away from that thought.

Ike crawled backwards. "How d'you think it got here? Was it somebody who wandered in and got lost?"

"Dunno. It's a kid, that's all you can tell. Too small for a grown-up."

"A kid? Like from that school?"

"School." It came together in Simon's head. "Remember that kid who was never found? What was his name? Jacob Redding. These could be his bones." He crawled to the front of the cave and stood up.

His knees felt squishy.

"But how'd he get down here?" Ike tore at his hair. "Oh, wait! Mystery solved! Remember what that book said about that special cell, the one they never found when they knocked the place down? What did they call it?"

"Buckingham Palace." Simon looked around at the walls, rough and stained and pressing too close. He stepped nearer to the door, which stood halfway open.

"So, they never found this cell because it was down here in the caves," Ike babbled, "not up there in the jail. But how could anybody do a thing like that to a kid? Put him down here and just leave him? M-maybe it wasn't on purpose. Maybe somebody put him here and just then the school was closed and he was, was, like, forgotten."

"But somebody knew. The person who put him here knew. And they didn't tell."

"I, I guess," Ike wobbled, "I guess they kept quiet about the boy because they knew they'd get in big trouble if anyone found out."

Simon knew Ike was trying not to think how bad this was. "So they just left him. Left him to die in the dark."

Ike made a sighing sound. "What can we do?"

"We can get his bones buried properly. Maybe find out for sure who he was. You know, DNA tests. Let's go."

"Right!" Ike scrambled to his feet and grabbed the flashlight. "But we haven't found the gate yet."

"Never mind the gate! I just want out!"

"Me too. But … gosh," Ike said, quietly for once. "Look."

He pulled the door almost closed. The flashlight beam moved slowly over the inner surface. "I can't see anything," Simon said. Then he caught his breath.

A picture was forming in the mottled, flaky surface. A hillside, a boy climbing, reaching up. The more he looked, the clearer the picture became. Now he could see the T-shirt and the shoes with stars on the ankles, and the star-shapes in the sky, although there was no red or gold or midnight blue, only reddish-brown rust. He could even make out the boy's hopeful expression.

"This is it!" Ike laughed. "Come on, aren't you going to open it?"

"Are you crazy?"

"But it shows you reaching for a star," Ike argued. "Reaching for a star, that means something good, right? It means you're just about to get something you really want."

"But who put my picture there? And why? The only reason I can see is to make me curious, so I'll open the gate. It's like — like cheese for a mouse!"

"But we've got a piece of Mythrin!" Ike begged. "The stone will take us there! It's like it was meant!"

Simon closed his hand on the stone in his pocket. "Who knows where it'll take us?"

"There's one way to find out." Ike held out his hand.

Simon clenched his fist around the stone for a moment. Then pulled it out. "I'll do it." He touched it to the rusty door. If this was a gate leading to Mythrin, the stone would open it.

They watched in silence. Simon was just starting to think that Ike was wrong and nothing was going to happen, when it happened. The gate began to form.

He thought of the other times he'd seen the world gate appear from behind its marker. How many times, six? Eight? It had always been so beautiful it had taken his breath away.

Not this time. This was no tall slab of sapphire blue, glowing like the evening sky. A slick brownish-greenish surface seeped forward from the rusty door, as if the iron was oozing mud.

Now the gate was fully formed. Its glistening green-brown-grey made Simon feel sick. The familiar twining shapes were there, but they looked like dead branches and rotting weeds.

And now he was supposed to touch the gate again, and the passage would open, and he and Ike would step in and the passage would zap them off to Mythrin.

Simon backed away. It was hard. The gate seemed to suck at him. He kept backing. His head hit the slanting roof.

Someone cried out: a faint sound from far away. He thought it came from behind the gate.

The gate stayed like that for what seemed an unnaturally long time. Simon began to be afraid it wouldn't close again, and they would be trapped here. *Because I can never go through that gate. Or even near it.* The distant cry came again: once, twice. Then the gate faded.

Simon gave the door a push with his foot and sidled out through the gap. Ike was three strides ahead of him. They headed back the way they'd come.

"Why is it so different from the other gates?" Ike wondered. "It looked like something gone bad. Like a rotten orange."

"Maybe it did go bad. Maybe that's what changed Ty and stole his memories. Did you, um, hear the voice?"

"What voice?"

"I heard somebody calling. From inside the gate, I thought."

"Nope. All I heard was my teeth rattling."

"I wonder if someone got stuck in there. Could that happen?"

Ike waved the flashlight in a dizzying way. "Who knows? It's a scientific challenge, right? We should find out what's going on."

"Yeah, well, I'm not going to experiment by going through that gate. No way. Not ever!"

Chapter 20

Rogue Mall

THEY CLIMBED the iron ladder one by one. It wasn't so bad this time. The ladder shook and creaked, but it held. "Still," Simon said, "I'm glad I won't be doing that again."

"Not going back in the caves? You're kidding!"

"Maybe once. To show the police where Jacob's bones are." Simon listened carefully with his ear against the OFF LIMITS door. He opened the door a crack and looked out. Then snuck out and led the way to the plywood barrier.

They watched and listened as they walked softly along the curve of the corridor. The mall cops and monitors didn't seem to be anywhere near, but something about the level had Simon poised to run.

"It's like the gate has let something out," he muttered. "This place is worse."

They walked down the middle of the corridor, staying away from the empty storefronts. The dusty windows shuddered slowly as they passed. As if, Simon thought, something large floated behind them, nosing at the glass. Ike pretended not to notice.

"Yowsers, am I thirsty," he said in his shiny-bright voice. He fished in a pocket for a toonie and veered towards the vending machines. Only one machine was lit up. It sold soft drinks and juice. Ike popped in the coin and punched the button for ginger ale.

Nothing happened for a moment. Then the coin return spat the coin back at him. He caught it and held it up. It was bent nearly in half.

"I guess it didn't like," Ike began. Then stepped back. The machine lit up all over, made a gronking sound like a mechanical goose, and started grinding towards him.

They raced for the escalator. It rose smoothly, but then Ike yelled and yanked at his right leg. "It's eating my pants!"

The edge of the escalator step was chomping on the frayed and trailing edge of Ike's jeans. "That's your fault, jackass!" Simon grabbed the pant leg and pulled. "Your jeans are always too long!"

He pulled Ike free. Ike leaped up the steps. "Run! Run!"

"Ike, this is just a machine! It doesn't want to eat you!" Simon felt a strange coldness at his toes. He looked down. The escalator's steel teeth had bitten off the ends of the rubber toe caps on his sneakers. Shreds of rubber were all over the step.

Simon bounded upward past the grinding teeth. At the top of the escalator he stopped short.

"Aha!" Ralston the Ratman was running towards them with the mall cops and the peer monitors at his back. "I told you I heard voices! That's them!"

Ike and Simon turned to run, but the guards caught them easily.

It wasn't good, but it could have been worse, as Ike said later. The guards didn't actually beat them up. They just shoved their pit-bull faces right up close and growled. They wanted Ty. Where was the blue-haired creep? How did he get in here? How did he get out?

Simon kept saying he didn't know. Ike kept yelling, "You just wait 'til the *Independent* gets hold of this!" Finally the guards picked them up, one each, slung them over a shoulder, and walked out the door with them. Then they tossed them. Ike and Simon landed hard and rolled.

Simon lay stunned for a minute, until a woman dressed in long,

125

old-fashioned clothes knelt beside him and helped him up. It was the weaver. "You okay?" she said. "That was nasty."

"They've gone strange." Simon remembered the escalators, and felt he ought to warn her. "The whole mall's gone strange. You better not go back in."

"Oh, I won't. They're throwing everybody out. I think they want the whole mall to themselves! Completely weird."

"It's like they've overdosed on *Soldier of Fortune* magazine," Ike said.

Simon looked at his watch, which, amazingly, was not broken. It said five-thirty. He couldn't believe it. With all that had happened, he felt it should be closer to midnight. "I better get home."

"Me too. I'm going to tell my dad how those goons roughed us up. That'll smoke their bacon!" Ike sighed. "Poor Ammy. Think of all the excitement she's missing!"

"Ammy!" Simon had forgotten all about her. "Right. I better phone her."

"UM, AMMY? Amelia, sorry. Listen. We've been under the mall, Ike and me. In the caves. And we found the gate."

"What? I didn't see anything like that in there! Where was it, exactly? How did you find it?"

"I'll start at the beginning." He described how he'd got mixed up in Ty's chase after the Ratman last night, and what Ty and John Lilac had said about the door with the starry window image. And finally how Ty had led them today to the hidden panel in the mall's lower level.

Ammy said nothing, so after a moment he went on to tell her how they'd climbed down the ladder into the caves, and found the cell with the bones, "and I'm sure they're Jacob Redding's bones. And the door of that cell was the world gate. It had my picture on it, just

126

like the starry window. Only in rust, not glass."

The phone was full of a crackling silence.

"Ammy?"

"Wait a minute. Ty told you about this?" There was a strange, choked sound in her voice.

"Y—"

"He *talked* to you?"

She was upset. Simon knew her well enough to know that. He just didn't understand why.

"Why would he talk with you and not with me?" she flared. "I'm his friend!"

Simon began to see. "Um, well, Ty just needed time to trust people enough to talk with them. And he needed to learn more language — remember, Mara didn't learn right away — and I just happened to be there at the right time. Otherwise, for sure it would have been you."

Couple of noisy breaths, then: "Okay. I've got to get there. I have to talk with him."

"You're coming down next weekend?"

"Weekend? No way! I'm coming now!"

"But you can't come now. There aren't any buses this late. And anyway your parents would never let you." Silence again. "Ammy?"

"Get it right for once! It's Amelia!" She hung up with a bang that hurt his ear.

CELESTE CAME home as he was hanging up the receiver. "Hello-o!" she sang out. "Are you in? Have I got something for you!"

"Uh, yes?" he said cautiously. With Celeste, you never knew.

She walked into the kitchen carrying a Doogie's Shoes box. Simon's heart sank.

"Guess who dropped by Boomer Heaven just now?" Celeste

plunked the box on the kitchen table. "Jean Dogood. She had three sizes of the same shoes. 'He obviously just loved them but said he couldn't afford them,' she said. 'So I'm offering them to you at a 50 per cent discount.' That's too good a deal to pass up!"

As she spoke, Celeste was busy unlidding the box, getting the shoes out, and pulling the wadded-up paper out of the toes. She laced them partway up. "There. It's time you had new shoes anyway. Look at the state of those you have on! The toes are all out!"

"Um, yes, but..." It would have been too hard to explain about the escalator, so he sat down on a chair by the table and tried on the new shoes while Celeste watched.

"They're, um." He stood up and shuffled around the kitchen floor. "They're too tight."

"Don't be silly!" Celeste bent down and poked the toes and squeezed the instep. "They're a perfect fit!"

Of course they fit. And of course it was no use pretending they didn't. Celeste always knew his shoe size better than he did, even though she didn't get it that he would never wear shoes like that.

Celeste picked up his toeless sneakers and carried them away to the trash. Simon went into his room to change into something else. But there was nothing else, except for the dress shoes she'd got him for somebody's wedding last year, and they were already too small. And his sandals, which — he dug them out and held them up — he couldn't wear. Ty had ripped the straps right out of the soles when he'd pulled them off on Saturday.

Simon sat on his bed and looked at the starry shoes at the far end of his legs. *Doomed.* Ike was right. The starry window was a prophecy, and it was trying to force Simon into doing something, or being something, that he didn't understand.

He made dinner: grilled cheese sandwiches. Celeste supervised. "Not the processed slices," she said. "The four-year-old cheddar. I'll chop the walnuts."

As they were doing the dishes, Celeste washing and Simon drying, the phone rang. Simon got it. "Oh, hi, Ike."

"You won't believe this! There's a riot at the mall!"

"A what?"

"Well, okay, an angry crowd. Seems lots of people complained about the way the mall guards were acting, and the police turned up. And the guards locked the doors."

"That's not hard to believe."

"Well, get this. Kevin and the quints are locked in there with them! They phoned their parents and said they won't come out until the cops promise they won't arrest the mall guys!"

"Oh, boy."

"And now their parents are all out by the mall, freaking out. My dad is covering the scene. I'll be watching from the bookstore roof. You coming?"

"If I can."

Simon hung up. "That was Ike. Can I go meet him?"

"All right. But don't be out past nine. And stay out of trouble!"

"You bet!"

When Simon knocked on the back door of the bookstore, Vesper answered. She frowned at him. "You too? This is not a theatre!" But she let him go up. He found Ike and John Lilac leaning on the brick parapet, looking down at the street. Ty sat cross-legged on the chimney.

"Welcome, friend," Lilac said in his deep, sombre voice. "Here's battle wrath o'erflowing. This night could see blood."

Simon leaned on the parapet next to Ike. It didn't look like a bloody scene. An OPP cruiser was parked across King Street. A knot of parents stood behind the car, watching the mall. Oscar Vogelsang was talking with them and writing in his notebook. Lisa Nader and

Bob Lebrun were at the mall entrance, trying to talk to somebody through the crack between the doors.

"We found the world gate in the caves underneath the mall," Simon told Lilac. "There's something wrong with it."

"Mayhap it wants your help. Why else would it show your likeness?"

"Dunno." Without thinking he added, "Maybe it wants to make another monster."

"Am I a monster, then?"

Simon looked at him cautiously. "Do you, um, feel like a monster?"

Lilac tilted his head back and forth, considering. "In the first days and weeks, yes. I was a monster in my own eyes. I always looked to see a different shape in the glass, yet knew not why. Not so now. This," and he held out a long, thin hand and turned it back and forth, "this is what I am. A man. The paragon of animals."

"Well, that's good, then," Simon said uncertainly.

Lilac turned from the parapet without another word and walked to the stairs. Simon watched him go. For someone who was okay with the way he was, there was a strange sadness in him.

Chapter 21

Buzzing the CN Tower

IT TOOK AMELIA half an hour to calm down. She paced her bedroom, kicked the furniture, and thought about the last time she'd seen Ty on Mythrin. The time he'd told her his real name. That was special. Names were important to the Urdar: Ty wouldn't tell just anybody.

That meant I was his friend. His special friend. He trusted me. And now look! He runs away from me. And he has conversations with Simon! It isn't fair!

Her chest hurt. She kicked the leg of her bed savagely. Then collapsed on the bed and rubbed her toes, sucking air though her teeth.

If only I could talk with him, I could get him to remember who he is — I'm sure of it! If only I could go there now, this minute! Like, on a transporter beam! That sounded so much like Ike that she flushed with shame.

"Think! How can I get to Dunstone now, and fast? There must be a way!"

She ticked them off in her head. Get her parents to drive her. No hope. Get them to let her take the bus. Less than no hope. Besides, Simon was right, there were no buses to Dunstone in the evening. And anyway, driving would take hours. Too long.

If only I could take a plane. If only Dunstone had an airport. But it doesn't. If only I could ... fly ...

131

Amelia sat perfectly still. Her heart thumped once, twice. Then she filled her lungs and leaped in the air and jumped up and down on the bed. "Yes!"

She bounced off the bed and bounded to the window. Then something Simon had said popped into her head and suddenly made sense. *I can't go in daylight. Somebody'll try to stop me. I'll have to wait until it's dark.*

After that it was hard to sit still. Impatience ate her up.

At six o'clock her father called her down to dinner. She wanted to refuse, couldn't eat, but knew that would be a mistake. They'd think she was sick and would want to check on her every fifteen minutes.

So she sat at the table, smiling absently and forking food into her mouth. It could have been gerbil casserole, for all she knew or cared.

"That was good!" She swallowed the last tasteless bite of dessert. "I'm totally full. Now I'm going upstairs to do my homework, okay?"

Silence. She looked up to see her parents gazing at her in a hopeful but puzzled manner. "I need to study for tests," she explained, smiling hard. "So don't bother looking in on me, okay? I may be up late."

She kept the smile firmly glued on as she carried her dishes to the kitchen, rinsed them, and put them in the dishwasher.

Back in her room, she turned on the light, closed and locked the door, and climbed out the window. Up the chain ladder to the roof.

The sun was just down, but there was still too much light. Amelia watched the last touch of gold melt off the apartment towers in the east. Behind them, Earth's purple shadow spread along the horizon.

At seven o'clock Amelia stood up between the chimneys. "Okay, I'll wait a few more minutes, to be on the safe side."

She closed her eyes. Mara, she thought. I've got to try and be like

Mara.

The thought sent a jolt of excitement along her veins. *Fire and steel. Smoke and diamond. That's me. Dragon.* She stretched her arms above her head and looked up and saw claws sprouting from her fingertips.

Oh, glory! This time I won't have to nearly kill myself!

The change came faster than ever before. So fast, Amelia realized her big dragon body was in danger of getting stuck in the space between the four chimneys. Still only half changed — head, arms and shoulders but not the rest — she leaped into the air.

No falling this time. She unfolded the wings that were suddenly there and with one downward stroke rose into the night sky. A long tail whipped around and walloped one of the chimneys. A brick knocked loose and crashed on the ground below.

Someone yelled. Between one wing stroke and the next, Amelia looked down and saw a slim figure standing on the driveway next to the house. It was Petra, with her mouth wide open. For the first time ever, Petra had lost her cool.

Amelia chortled. Then she thought, there goes my only chance at a real human friend. But right now she was so chock-full of joy, there was no room left for sadness. She turned her head and winked, knowing Petra would see the shine of the dragon eye.

She circled up, higher and higher, wider and wider, south over roofs and roads and beaches and out over the glimmering expanse of Ashbridges Bay. And then a wide wheeling swoop and she was flying west, towards the orange glow of the horizon. Towards Dunstone.

And straight towards the CN Tower.

AMELIA HAD BEEN up in the CN Tower one summer five years ago. Celeste said it was something every tourist had to do, once.

It was Simon's first and only time, too. He'd been too scared to

133

walk on the glass floor where you could look down at the tiny parked cars a thousand feet below. Amelia had been nice enough not to laugh at him, even though the glass floor never scared her.

The thing she'd really loved about the tower had been the revolving restaurant. They'd sat there eating grilled chicken and mocha crunch ice cream, watching the tops of skyscrapers slide past far below.

They'd watched planes take off from the Island Airport, too. Looking down from above on the flying airplanes had made Amelia feel amazingly powerful, as if she, too, were flying.

And now she really was. Toronto's nightscape lay below, a bewildering blaze of gold and silver, ruby and emerald. The CN Tower stuck up out of the blaze, taller and taller as she flew nearer. She could see the elevator running up the outside of the shaft like a firefly on a string. She could see the revolving restaurant, a golden band around the pod near the top, and then she could see the shapes of people through the slanted windows.

And then she was there, veering around the tower. Stunned-looking faces stared out at her. The voice in her head that sounded like Simon told her that what she was doing was stupid and dangerous. Another voice in her head that sounded like Ty laughed and laughed. She opened her jaws in a bright dragon smile.

She only circled once. The tower whizzed by too fast for her to see much. The people just sat there, as if they'd turned to ice. All except a little blond girl, maybe five, who plastered herself to the glass and beamed out at her. And an old man who raised a glass in salute as the dragon flowed past.

And then the tower was behind her. The glittering city slid below. She found the Gardiner Expressway, a river of moving lights, and followed it to what she guessed was Mississauga, because of the airplanes taking off away to the north. Better stay away from there!

Even a dragon might have trouble messing with a jumbo jet.

Sooner than she expected, the glittering floor began to show dark patches. She crossed the bright ribbon of Highway 401 and then she was out over the light-spangled countryside.

It all skimmed by so fast she hardly had time to see where she was going. *How fast am I flying?* She looked down. Faster than those cars down on the highway, wow! A glow of lights crept up to her right, far ahead, and slid towards her. That had to be Guelph, judging by the 401, which was now on her left.

Better head a bit more south. Then after Guelph, more north. Stay away from the cities.

The glow of Guelph slid away and another bright glow grew to the left, ahead. Kitchener. Nearly there! Amelia danced mid-air for sheer joy, cartwheeled, did a few barrel rolls just to make herself excitingly dizzy, and then flew on.

Maybe it was the barrel rolls that did it. Or maybe it was the dinner she'd shovelled in without thinking. Or both. That dessert, she recalled now in full-colour detail, had been a large wedge of lemon meringue pie with a chocolate crust.

Amelia groaned. Remind *me next time not to fly on a full stomach.* Her belly felt hot, as if the pie was cooking inside it. It churned. *Oh no....* Amelia wondered what dragon barf would do to people, if it landed on them. Would it burn like acid?

She tried to keep it inside. It wasn't working. A big, hot bubble pushed up from inside. *Got to let it out!*

Amelia did her best. She made sure the glitter of Kitchener stayed on her left. She waited until there was nothing below but darkness, not even the lights of a farm. Then she opened her jaws.

"Whoa!"

It wasn't barf. Or maybe it had been once, but now it was fire, a long plume of white-hot flame bursting across the sky. Right under

135

her nose, a small airplane dipped and swerved. A face looked out of the cockpit. It seemed to be yelling. Then it was gone.

Amelia circled to look back. The plane was a pattern of coloured lights shrinking towards Toronto. No harm done. She recalled now that there was an airport on the edge of Kitchener. *Oh, well. I can't keep track of everything!*

After that her stomach felt much better. She flew on. Now the big cities lay behind. Below lay swaths of darkness speckled with tiny lights and threaded with silver rivers.

Ahead, soon, Dunstone. And there it was! Amelia was getting good at recognizing things from the air. That had to be Dunstone over there, it was the right size cluster of lights. From up here it was a scatter of gold tucked into folded valleys.

She circled in wide and high. Rooftops sped past far below. She opened her mind to the cloud of thoughts that floated over Dunstone. It billowed up at her, soft and grey-violet-pink. One thought flared like blue-green flame.

Ty! Wait there! I'm coming!

Amelia held Ty's thought and followed it down and down. With a skid and a scatter of gravel, she landed on the roof of a building. Simon was there, and Ike. They were just turning around as if they had been leaning on the parapet, watching the street below.

And there was Ty, jumping down from a chimney. He turned to run.

Amelia flashed back to human form. "Ty! Ty, please! Don't you remember? It's me, Amelia!"

Ty took a running leap, cleared the gap between the buildings, and bounded off across the roofs into the night.

Chapter 22

Hatchling

AMELIA FELL into a heap on the roof. She shook her fists in the air and howled with frustration. "Ty! Come back!"

No!

She looked around. There was no sign of him, but the bright thread of his thought still glimmered across her mind. He hadn't cut her off. She could picture him hunkered down somewhere out there in the dark: nervous, curious, listening.

Simon touched her shoulder. "You okay?"

"Yeah, I'm great." She brushed his hand off and thought of Ty.

"You were a dragon? You flew here? All the way from Toronto?"

"Yes! Shh! I'm trying to get to Ty."

She closed her eyes and touched the thread of thought. *Ty! Please come back.*

What are you?

Friend. Amelia. You know me.

No . . . That sounded less certain.

Ardin child, you called me. We flew together.

I flew? How?

Like this.

She pulled out the memory — it was one she would never, ever forget — and shoved it in his direction as hard as she could. How they'd sped over the ocean of Mythrin, wingtip to wingtip. She with the Prism Blade, the dragons' Great Bane, gripped in her back claws. He with the knowledge of where to hide it so it would never be found again.

How they flew and flew. The steady beat of wings, the smooth glide of muscles, the rush of cool wind past her ears. Sea shimmering below, sun blazing above. *I could fly like this forever,* she'd said. *I too,* he'd answered.

Suddenly the memory was gone and she was alone, but still flying, still high above the sea. She coasted down to land on a rocky beach below tall cliffs. Gulls shrieked. Stones rolled and clacked under her feet. A thick, strong cord, a rope of blue-green light, snaked across the beach and into a crevice in the cliff face.

This is like a dream, Amelia thought.

Then: Not *like* a dream, it *is* a dream. A dragon dream, where things are more real than real. *I'm inside Ty's head.*

At last she understood. Ty was lost inside his own dreaming mind. She had to bring him out.

Finding him, at least, would not be a problem. The thread of his thought was even stronger now, easier to see. Amelia followed the shining cord into the crevice, up the twisting path of a gully, and onto a windswept hilltop. Then she took to the air.

The country of Ty's dream was a vast and tangled wilderness. A beautiful, wild, and dangerous land: like Ty himself, Amelia thought. There were long-grass prairies, miles of wind-rippled silvery green. Deep ravines with waterfalls crashing down. Forests thick and black, where dappled deer ran in the shadows and lean grey wolves looked up with shining eyes.

The forest ended suddenly. Amelia's shadow winged over a carpet of low purple shrubs, then white rocks, and then — nothing. The land stopped. Glancing back, she saw a cliff so tall that its crest rose above drifting clouds.

A bright blue sea lay far below and stretched to the horizon. She sailed down and down until the waves splashed her stomach. The cord of Ty's thought ran ahead to an island, a heap of rock that grew to a mountain as she came nearer.

She crossed a beach, followed the cord in and out of caves and crevasses, crawled through mazes of tumbled boulders, twirled around pinnacles.

It struck her that Ty had gone to a lot of trouble to hide himself. Something must have scared him badly. What could do that? She used to think Ty wasn't scared of anything at all.

Just as she was beginning to think this winding trail would never end, she climbed out onto a wide shelf below the island's highest peak. Ty's thought-cord melted away in the sun. The link was gone.

"So this is the end."

Amelia's big body sagged onto the shelf. A wide blue ocean spread out below. It would have been good to rest here, if she hadn't just lost Ty. Good to watch the spiralling birds, to sleep on the sun-warmed rocks.

Sleep, she thought longingly. Turning to fit her body to the curve of the rocks, she spotted what she thought at first was a bright blue rock.

At second glance it was a tiny turquoise dragon, curled up asleep in a warm hollow with its tail over its eyes. A baby, a hatchling no bigger than Amelia's front paw.

"Ty!" Amelia did a shuffling dance. "I've found you! But why are you so small?"

The tiny dragon slept on.

"Ty! Wake up!"

He let out a mouse-sized snore. Amelia gently rocked him from side to side. She blew in his ear. He slept on.

She sat back, ready to flame with frustration. Why wouldn't he wake up? He'd told her his name once, his true name. And now he wouldn't even...

His true name.

Names had power, she knew that from Mara. A dragon's name spelled out his family tree and his place in the world. But more than that: it was a key to his heart and mind, his weakness and strength. It was himself.

Amelia lowered her jaws to the sleeping hatchling's ear. She whispered: "Tynenannarrithen."

The tiny creature stirred. His head lifted. He opened his eyes, and they were Ty's golden eyes. He blinked up at her.

"Hello, Tynenannarrithen."

He made a cheeping sound, like a sparrow.

"Come on, then. I'm going home and you're coming with me."

Ty cheeped again and stood up. He took a few tottery steps.

"My gosh! You must be really young. Guess I'm lucky you didn't get scared right back into the egg. Poor bitty thing."

Amelia picked him up and tucked him into the crook of her left elbow. He nestled in and clung on with sharp little claws. Then she leaped from the shelf, circled the island, and headed back towards the tall cliff and the tangled wilderness beyond.

Ty started to get heavy as they flew above the forest. Amelia glanced down at him, and he was certainly bigger. He was the length of her forearm now. His tail curled around her elbow. He rested his jaw on her wrist and peered down at the crumpled tree-carpet rippling past far below.

Funny. Why would he be growing?

At just about the same time, Amelia realized she had no idea what direction to go. There was no thought thread to guide her.

She winged on. Now the trees were gone and a dark plain stretched to the horizon all around. There were no waterfalls, no silvery-green grasslands. Ty grew heavier and heavier. He started to slide off her arm and dug in his claws, which were now much larger and stronger.

"Ow! This isn't working!" Amelia spiralled down and landed on a plain covered with wiry grass.

The young dragon leaped off her arm and rolled a few times, then jumped up and fanned his wings. He lurched into the air and tumbled back. He sat up again and laughed a creaky dragon laugh. Then he tried flying again. Fell down again.

Words bounced across Amelia's mind. *I can I can I can I can,* Ty was saying.

"Ty! You're growing up!"

That had to be good. Maybe it meant he was starting to come out of hiding. "If only you could lead us home."

It was getting dark, and it didn't look as if there would be stars in that blank grey sky. Soon they would both be lost, and then how would they ever get out?

Ty raised his snout and sniffed. He wrinkled his nose. *Ew!*

"What?" Amelia sniffed. This place smelled like damp rocks and earth and green things. "Nothing bad about.... Wait a sec ...." She snuffled the air. Here was something different. A thin, cold breeze. It carried a trace of wood smoke, and .... She widened her nostrils, inhaled.

Wood smoke. Mouldering leaves. Oily pavement. Gasoline fumes. And — yes — fresh doughnuts!

Dunstone!

"Ty! Come on!" She grabbed him by the spike on the back of his neck and pulled him along beside her. Soon she didn't need to pull him. He ran beside her, and he grew as he ran. The wiry grass crunched under their feet.

The smell of home grew stronger. Now there was sound, too: a train whistle, soft and lonesome with distance. Amelia laughed and spat out a small flare. Ty leaped high and was suddenly airborne. This time he didn't fall. Amelia sprang into the air beside him. He turned his head and shone his eyes at her.

Amelia! It's you!

The dark dreamland vanished. Cold air burst in Amelia's face. Wingtip to wingtip, they soared out over the roofs of Dunstone.

Chapter 23

Ty Tells a Tale

"TRYING TO GET to Ty," she'd said. To Simon, it looked as if Ammy had just sat down and closed her eyes. He had time to exchange a puzzled look with Ike and get a reassuring grip on the Mythrin stone. And then things exploded.

From one breath to the next, Ammy was gone. Next breath, a big red-brown dragon burst out of the night, right beside an even bigger blue-green dragon, and the two of them flashed overhead and rocketed up into the black sky.

Ike jumped up and down and punched the air. "Yes! She did it!"

Simon scanned the sky. "We're lucky it's so dark." He could just make out the flicker of a wing across the hazy stars.

Ike craned his neck back. "How long d'you think they'll stay up there? We need Ty to report on that gate under the mall."

Gravel scattered behind them. Two enormous dragon shapes lit down on the roof and folded their wings. You couldn't tell anything from their armour-plated faces, but their eyes shone with joy.

"I am back!" Ty trumpeted. "I am myself again!" He lifted his head and inhaled.

"Stop!" Ammy fluted. "We'll have the firefighters up here!"

Ty choked and coughed, and belched a small flare that couldn't have been seen from the next roof, let alone the street.

Simon walked over and stood under the two big, shining snouts. They grinned down at him. "We need to talk," he said.

"Talk, then." Ty's grin widened. Simon had forgotten how big and sharp dragon teeth were. Those jaws would make a one-bite snack of him.

Ty had grown since the last time they'd seen him. He wasn't a teenager any more. He was a full-grown dragon, or almost, and he probably didn't think much of puny little ardin kids.

Simon squared his shoulders. "I need you two to be in human shape."

The two dragons looked at each other. They had to be using mind-talk. Of course they knew how annoying that was.

"All right," Ammy-dragon said at last. And in next to no time, she stood there in her own shape.

Ty tossed his head. "Must I?" He looked at Ammy again. "This feels so good. It has been so long."

"Please." She touched his clawed hand. "Just for a little while."

Ty blew a hot sigh across the roof, then settled into human shape. Not the mohawk haircut and leathers and chains he'd worn last summer at the Dunstone and Area Weird Games. He'd kept the green-blue hair, but now it stood up in gelled points all over his head. That cleared his eyes, and now they were real dragon eyes, glinting gold, with cat-like vertical pupils. He looked like a tall, blue-tipped flame.

What surprised Simon was that Ty was still wearing the jeans and hoodie and T-shirt they'd given him, all cleaned up and good as new. No, better than new. The jeans fit now. The DAWG T-shirt was a brighter red, with the inscription ("Proud to be a DAWG") and the dopey-looking hound cartoon even crisper than before.

Ike walked all around him, staring. "How do you do that? I mean, what happens to the clothes you wear when you change? Do they get kind of mushed into your DNA?"

Ty smiled gently. "I remember you. You are the little ardin I was planning to eat."

"Aha. Joke." Ike edged closer to the stairwell door.

"Ty," Simon said quickly. "Tell us how you got here. And what changed you? Um, please. If you don't mind."

Ty paced around the roof, stretching his legs and limbering his shoulders. "Oh, to fly again!" he sighed. Then he leaped to a chimney and settled down, cross-legged, next to the flue. It didn't seem to bother him that there was smoke and probably scorching air rising out of it. "Listen, then," he said, "and I will tell you the tale."

THINK BACK, Ty said, to the time when Mara warred with her brother, Ty's father. "I will not name him; we will call him Tarq." Defeated, Tarq and most of his followers chose exile. They flew overseas, found an empty land, and settled near a ruined city of the gate makers on a sheltered bay of the sea.

Five years passed. In that time, Tarq's thirst for revenge cooled. He saw that his people could make a life here. He grew wiser. He became a good leader.

But then Zeph appeared.

"You remember that old snake Zephrinarrinaden?" Ty spat. "He who would have killed half the dragons of Mythrin so he could rule the rest!"

After Zeph's defeat, he too flew overseas and joined the colony. One day, he persuaded Tarq to explore the ardin ruins with him. Tarq was never seen again. Zeph said they had found an evil gate that sucked Tarq in before Zeph could save him.

Zeph joined the others in their fiery mourning. Soon after, he was chief. Most said he was the right choice: he was clearly the oldest, biggest, strongest, and wisest dragon in the colony.

But in the three years that followed, he changed. He no longer listened to the ideas of others. He stopped even pretending to listen.

He did not like to be questioned.

The other dragons avoided the ardin city, but Zeph went there often. He found machines, and forced some of his followers to try them out. Some of those dragons died.

"You see why?" Ty said. "Zeph was seeking another weapon like the Prism Blade, one that he could use against our chief. Even now, he wants to rule the world!"

When a small group led by Pirrip, Tarq's oldest friend, stood up against Zeph and demanded a muster, Zeph did a monstrous thing. He called a muster, which by age-old custom is a time when anyone can speak, but no-one can fight. And at the muster, Zeph and his followers attacked Pirrip's group and killed them, all except one.

Pirrip alone escaped. Wounded, he flew back overseas, a slow eight-day trip from island to island, to ask for help. Ty and a friend, "we'll call him Shinyblack," found Pirrip collapsed on the shore. Hearing his story, Ty decided to fly overseas to find out for himself. Shinyblack stayed behind to take the message to Mara.

Ty, impatient as always, flew straight across the sea. He flew for three days, with brief rests on small rocks and floating logs.

"I never slept. Of course, that was my mistake. When I reached the other side, I was too tired to guard my thoughts. And when Zeph found me, I was too tired to fight. He took me and set a cage around my mind and flew with me to the ardin city and pushed me into the gate. And so I came here. And when I came I was changed, and lost. Until you found me."

AFTER TY finished speaking there was a long silence. Ammy was the first to break it. "Wow!" she said. "That's amazing!"

Ty jumped down from the chimney. "Not. I was a fool. I should have waited for our chief. See what trouble I got myself into!"

Ike, who had been busy with the calculator on his iphone, slipped it back in his pocket. "It works out. It sounds like a bit less than eight years have gone by on Mythrin since Simon and Ammy came back that first time, last January. On Earth it's been 294 days. The 9.5-to-1 time ratio still holds!"

"So now we know for sure there's a gate under the mall that goes to the overseas land on Mythrin," Ammy said. "But can we use it?"

Ty shook his head sharply. "You ardini, maybe. I only know I will never go back that way. Never!"

Simon walked to the parapet and looked down at the street. The police were back at their car. Lisa Nader was talking into a phone. Several of the parents were shouting. One man, Simon thought it was Kevin's father, was waving a tire iron and pointing at the mall's glass doors. Bob Lebrun was trying to get him to hand over the tire iron. Oscar was taking their picture.

"Things are getting worse," Simon said. "It's the gate."

"The gate!" Ike laughed. "How do you figure that?"

"Remember that chemical dump they found outside town last year?"

"From that old factory? Right. They were going to build houses there, and they couldn't, because of the poison in the ground."

"This is like that." Simon thought of the muddy sheen of the gate. "Only, it's poisoning people's minds instead of their bodies. We've got to stop it! Get them to close the mall. Fill in the caves. Before something really bad happens."

Ammy took hold of Ty's arm. "Maybe Mara can do something."

"The chief may be overseas by now," he said. "If Zeph is harming his people, our chief can't leave them to suffer. She would go there to challenge him."

"So we have to go there too!" Ammy shook his arm.

"Yes, but — "

Ty suddenly spun around to face the stairwell door. There hadn't

147

been any sound that Simon heard, but the door was open and John Lilac stood there. He was watching Ty.

Ty gazed back at him and then dipped his head in a salute. "It is you."

"You know me, then? What am I? What are you?"

"I am a warrior of the Urdar," Ty said softly, as if not to frighten away a bird perched on his hand. "So are you. We are dragons. You are my father."

Chapter 24

A Voice in the Passage

SIMON WAS NOT surprised. Once you'd heard Ty's story, it was obvious who John Lilac had to be. Zephrinarrinaden had joined the exiles and almost at once he'd put Tarq through the gate. That was three years ago, Mythrin time: early July this year, Earth time. Exactly when Vesper Wynn had found a nameless man in the gorge.

They all looked at John Lilac. He frowned and shook his head.

"Look at your hands," Simon said. "The extra joints."

"And the things you did," Ike chimed in. "Like, how you made everything stop, and made Simon think he'd gone blind. Mind things."

"I did not!" Lilac took a step backward.

"Stay!" Ty called. "Amelia freed me with my name. I know your name, your true name. I will speak it." He said nothing Simon could hear, just looked.

Lilac flinched. "Stop!" He clawed at his head.

"You're hurting him," Simon said. "Ammy? Can't you go in and bring him out, the way you brought Ty out?"

"Maybe. Only if he lets me."

Lilac dropped his hands. "I am who I am. I am John Lilac."

"But that's just it — you're not!" Ammy waved her hands at him. "You're a dragon! Wouldn't you rather be a dragon than human?"

"I am John Lilac," he said fiercely. "I do not want you ramping about in my mind."

"The chief could heal him," Ty said. "She healed others. There was a dragon whose mind went wandering when a boulder fell on his head, and she brought it back. A true chief is a healer, and she is a true chief. Perhaps she can heal him while helping us to fix that gate."

"But how can we get to Mythrin?" Ike demanded. "Mr. Manning's gate is out. The one in the gorge is under heaps of rock. The one under the mall—"

"I will not use," Ty sliced in.

"There's no other way," Ike said.

Ammy suddenly jumped and clapped her hands like a kid. "Oh, yes there is! There's the gate from the window in the old library!"

Simon shook his head. That gate had been beyond their reach since last summer, when the library was knocked down. "We can't use that. It's fifteen feet up in the air."

"No problem!" Ty flexed an arm and began to shape a wing.

"And invisible."

"Not to a dragon!" Ty's body lengthened. His arms went down to the ground. His hands grew claws.

"Yes! This is great!" Ike shook his fists in the air. "Mythrin, here we come!"

"All right, then. Everybody ready?" Simon looked at John Lilac, who was staring at Ty's uncoiling tail. "Um, Tarq?"

"My name is not Tarq!"

"But it isn't Lilac, either," said a new voice.

They all looked. Vesper Wynn stood at the top of the stairs, a small figure almost hidden behind John Lilac. He turned sideways to look at her.

"I gave you that name because of your eyes," she said. "I always knew there was something different about you. I always hoped I would help you find out who … what … you really are."

150

"But if I do," he said slowly, "will I forget John Lilac? Will I forget you, and this place?" He waved around at the bookstore under him and the sky above. "I don't want to forget."

"Well, that's — good to hear. But you ought to know who you are. You should go." She cleared her throat and crossed her arms.

"I will come back if I can."

"Don't make any promises!"

"No more talk," Ty said. "Come! Come now!"

Things moved fast after that. Ammy changed. Lilac climbed onto Amelia's shoulders. Simon and Ike sat on Ty, who was bigger and stronger.

They lifted off with a stomach-dropping surge. Vesper waved and was gone. Roof shapes and the silvery snake of the gorge skimmed beneath. A few wing-strokes and they were circling above the empty lot where the old library used to be. The river churned and roared beside it.

Simon couldn't see anything in the air, but Ty darted his head and next moment a tall, glowing, sapphire-blue door formed with nothing to hold it up. They flew in wide circles while the door changed from a jewel-like slab covered with twining shapes to a passage punched into the heart of twilight. They plunged through, Ammy first.

Just as he fell into the glowing passage, it struck Simon that he was still wearing the starry shoes. And Ty, somewhere in his DNA, still wore the red T-shirt. And they were together.

But in the passage, Simon no longer worried about anything. His mind was clear and calm. He wondered again what this place was, this passage between the gates: what it was for, and who had made it.

He floated in blueness and wondered if time was passing at all, and why he seemed to be alone here. He couldn't see or hear Ike or Ty. He only had his thoughts. Not even a body. Thinking this, he tried to look at his hands, but couldn't find them. There was nothing to feel or hear or see but the singing blue.

Sparks of light leaped in sizzling arcs from point to point through the blueness. Like in a brain, he thought. Like neurons. Electrical messages. Suddenly he thought he understood. The gates, the gates and passages were ....

Simon.

The voice again! But wait, that voice belonged in another gate, a different passage. What was it doing here?

Simon!

Someone calling his name. Calling for him. It wasn't Ty or Ike or Ammy.

Simon! Please help! It was a young voice: a boy's voice.

Who are you? he called back.

Next moment the twilight passage vanished and he shot out into brilliant sunshine.

Chapter 25

Many Doors

AMELIA DANCED and flipped. Someone shouted in her ear. She remembered her passenger. "Sorry!"

But she felt too wonderful to be sorry. This was Mythrin! She'd forgotten how clean the air was, fresh enough to shock your lungs. She skimmed across a valley and over a chattering stream, and dropped down on the far hillside.

A sharp aroma rose around her. She remembered the yellow-flowered bushes, how the tough stems whipped your ankles. The low-slanting sunlight set the hillside glowing.

John Lilac slid from her back and stood looking around and shaking.

Ty settled nearby. Ike whooped with excitement. Simon wore that blank look that meant he was thinking of three things at once. Ty gave a shake and the boys slid off in a flurry of yells and arms and legs.

They picked themselves up and then they all walked down the hill, with John Lilac silently bringing up the rear. A grassy meadow lay on the other side of the noisy stream, where Pier and her people had made their camp.

Amelia looked around. There was no sign now that humans had ever been here, not even the ashes of a cooking fire. Then she looked up.

"What happened to the cliff?" she said. "Where's the Hall of

Gates?"

"That's what I was going to ask," Simon asked. "We should have come out of the gate into a building. Where is it?"

The Hall of Gates was a tall building that used to stand on a ledge halfway up the cliff. It had been there before the dragons came to Mythrin, thousands of years ago. Inside, a dozen or so gates linked Mythrin to other worlds, their places marked by coloured glass windows set in the stone walls.

One of those gates had brought Amelia and Simon here last June, Earth time, from the gate in the old library, and the same gate had brought them here today. Now the Hall of Gates was gone. The ledge had collapsed into a slope of tumbled rock. Bits of colour winked among the stones. Simon crunched over and picked up a shard of ruby-red glass.

"Dragons did it," Ty said in his bright trumpet voice. "We could not close the gates, so we tried to bury the hall. The mountain broke."

"Like breeds like!" Ike jogged on the spot. "Remember how the old Dunstone Library got demolished? This is just like that!"

Simon gazed upward, shading his eyes against the sun. "That's a problem. Now we can't see if the starry window is there."

"*I* can see the windows." Amelia couldn't resist. "That's my dragon sight, of course."

Simon put on his most patient look. "Ammy — Amelia — the windows were just the markers to show where the actual gates are. They were just lead and glass." He held up the broken piece of red glass to show her. "They are now in bits on the ground. You can't see— "

"I *can* see them! Plain as day! Ty, can't you?"

Ty wagged his head from side to side. "Yes and no. They are like pictures in water."

"There, you see?"

"I guess that's possible," Simon said grudgingly. "Can you see the starry window?"

"Can't tell from here." She leaped into the air and flapped across the valley towards the broken mountain. Ty flew beside her.

She wouldn't admit it to Simon, of course, but the windows were *not* plain as day. In fact, if she hadn't been staring at the spot, she might not have noticed them. Looking at them close up, the double row of tall, round-topped oblongs were faint as cloud. It was as if the windows had died and these were their ghosts.

Their jewel-like colours had faded to watery pastels. But you could still see the pictures, if you looked really hard. Fanning her wings just enough to stay aloft, she floated along the outside of the double row. She remembered all these. There was the one they'd just come through, the one with the warrior battling the huge, coiling snake.

Others showed men and women fighting with monsters. One showed a crowned woman holding a skull. One showed a green dragon with a chain wrapped around its neck. (Ty snarled at that one.)

They flew all around the double row of ghost-windows. Then they glided back down to the valley. Simon and Ike had crossed the stream by the stepping-stones. John Lilac was slowly following them.

"Well?" Simon demanded.

"Not there." Amelia folded her wings. "And yes, I'm sure."

Simon looked at Ike. "It was there last summer. I saw it."

"So it moved to Dunstone," Ike said. "Or did it? My theory is—"

Amelia felt her stomach getting hot. She vented a steamer of flame above their heads. "Enough with the geek talk!"

"Yes, we came here to find the chief," Ty said. "Where is everyone?" *Is there no guard on these gates?* he called out in mind-speech.

I am here! carolled a strange voice in Amelia's head, which she guessed must be sounding in Simon's head too, and Ike's and Lilac's, because they all looked up, startled. *I went only to hunt for lunch. I am coming!*

Ty leaped into the air, trumpeting joyfully. A name flitted from his head so fast Amelia knew she wasn't meant to catch it, and she also knew it would have been rude to try. She looked around, and a dragon soared over the seaward rim of the valley and swooped down at them.

Ty met him in the air and the two of them danced and twirled and batted at each other with their tails. The other one was glossy black like patent leather. Amelia thought: they're like a couple of guys horsing around because they feel so great about meeting again.

Ty glided down to land in the meadow next to the river. Shinyblack settled nearby and looked the others over. *That one is strange.* He pointed a claw at John Lilac. *He is Urdar and not Urdar. His mind is like a stone. He frightens me.*

Lilac sat down among the yellow-flowered shrubs. He dropped his head into his hands.

As for me, said Shinyblack, still broadcasting for all to hear, *when the chief found I had not stopped you from flying overseas, she set me to watch these gates as punishment.*

She was angry? Ty sounded worried.

Oh, yes. Shinyblack flicked his tail. *But mostly at you.*

When did she leave? Amelia put in.

She is gone now for thirty days. She took only twenty with her, her personal followers.

"So she's not planning war." Simon's human voice broke into the lightning-quick zigzag of mind-talk.

Not war, Shinyblack said. *Something I do not understand. Chiefs' talk.*

156

"Diplomacy," John Lilac said in a muffled voice from behind his hands.

Simon touched him gingerly on the shoulder. "Um, are you all right? Are you starting to remember?"

Lilac clutched his head again. *In pieces. Like broken glass.* "It hurts." He pulled up a handful of yellow blossoms and crushed them, then inhaled the fragrance. "Home, and yet strange," he muttered. *Shuffled with my Earth memories.* "Side by side, over and under." *I will go mad.*

Shinyblack took a few careful steps away from him. He looked at Ty. *Will you stay here until she returns?*

No. Ty arched his neck, ready for action. *We must go after her, but we must go the fast way, not the safe way. We will fly straight across the ocean.*

"Wait a minute!" Ike hugged his stomach. "That takes three days! We'll starve!"

"You will not!" Ty wheezed with laughter. "There are fish."

"Okay," Simon said, "but how do we know you and Ammy can fly there carrying a load of us? It was hard enough with nobody on your back, remember?"

"What other way is there?" Amelia put in.

"Phooey!" Ike waved his arms around at the valley. "You'd think the gate makers would have built gates connecting two places on their own world, wouldn't you? I mean, if they could connect two worlds in different universes, two places on one world would've been easy-peasy."

"Maybe they did," Simon said, "but guessing doesn't help us any."

There is... Shinyblack had been bobbing around them, trying to slip a word in. *There is a gate like that.* They all looked at him.

No joke? How do you know? Ty's thoughts vibrated with

157

excitement.

Our chief went by that gate. It is a way known only to chiefs. But she told me where it is, in case you found your way back here. Come, I can take you there.

Chapter 26

A Chief of the Urdar

THE GATE KNOWN only to chiefs was northward, up the coast. By the time they reached the spot, the sun had gone down behind the hills in the west. They found a wall of smooth black rock at the back of a ledge overlooking the sea.

The ledge was wide open. But Amelia could see how these gates had remained secret. The smooth black wall looked blank until you ran a hand over it and found the thin grooves cut into the rock. Then you saw how the grooves outlined a row of three tall, round-topped door-shapes. Even then they were hard to see.

That one. Shinyblack pointed a claw at the door-shape in the middle.

AT THE OTHER END the gate tipped them out into middle-of-the-night darkness. Mythrin's little sequin moon gleamed down at them.

Simon shuffled his new glitzy sneakers, which looked all wrong on him, and cleared his throat. "Did, um, anyone notice anything different in the passage?"

"Like what?" Ike was running his hands along the grooved outlines of the doors.

"Like, the light wasn't as bright?"

"Come to think of it...." Amelia felt a pang of worry. "Yeah. What does that mean?"

"Probably just that this is a local gate," Ike said cheerfully. "It

159

wouldn't use as much energy as a gate between worlds. Less energy, light not so bright."

"I hope you're right," Simon said. But he didn't look much happier. "I suppose nobody heard that voice calling, except me? Okay, never mind."

They stood on a wide platform cut into a mountainside. Amelia and Ty perched on the edge of the shelf. "Whoa!" Amelia called. "Come look at this!"

Right below them, ghostly in the silvery-blue moonlight, the forest stepped down and down to a great city that lay in the lap of the mountains around the curve of an ocean bay. A black and white city, with sharp towers that glittered like needles, and one tower at the centre that rose half as high as the hills.

"A city of the gate makers!" Ike rolled up his eyes. "I'm in heaven! Imagine what we'll find down there!"

"You will find nothing." John Lilac's deep voice startled them all. "I remember this. Most is broken rock and trees. The shining bits are stone that seems to live, yet is dead. The poisoned gate is down there."

They were all silent, even Ike. Then Amelia gave herself a shake and made her tail-spikes clash. "Well, we're not here to poke around in old ruins. We're here to find Mara."

"Yes," Ty said. "And I feel she is near." His eyes brightened, and then Amelia heard it too: that unmistakable voice in her head. *Get down here this instant!*

Chief! Ty warbled. *I am here! I have come back from the dead! And I bring—*

I know who you bring. Look up, all of you! You are in danger!

Amelia looked up. Black shapes flickered over the stars. She made out a long line of dragons flying towards them over the ruined city. There were at least a dozen.

160

Simon thumped Amelia on the forearm. "What's the matter? Where's Mara?"

Ty gazed at the oncoming dragons. *These are not my people.*

They are too many to fight. Amelia was really afraid he would try it. The Ty she remembered would have hurled himself at them, screaming. But this Ty was what, three years older? Time enough to grow some sense.

All that passed through her mind in the half-second before Ty said, *You are right. We fly away to fight another day.*

The line of dragons was still maybe ten wing beats away, but they were slanting downward. *They mean to cut us off,* Ty said.

We'll make it. Si and Ike and John won't.

Yes, they will! Ty picked up Ike in his clawed left fist and Simon in his right. Amelia grabbed John Lilac under the arms. A flick of the wing and they were in the air. Treetops brushed Amelia's feet.

Down! Ty shouted. *Into the woods!*

He plunged, and Amelia followed. Branches tore loose, leaves showered down. They landed in a clearing with barely enough room for humans to move; no room at all for dragons.

Change! Ty dropped Ike and Simon into some bushes that must have been full of thorns, judging by the yells. Amelia set John Lilac down on his feet and changed back to human. When she looked around, Ty was pulling the two boys out of the bushes.

Something flicked overhead. There was a gap in the forest canopy where they'd barrelled through. More dragons passed over it, blurs against the starry sky. A couple of seconds and they'd be landing on the ledge. And then they'd be down here.

No need to talk it over. They scrambled. Ty led the way down the hill and deeper under the cover of the trees, breaking a path for the others through the dense undergrowth. The woods were a maze of shadows. John Lilac moved easily but Simon and Ike stumbled along,

161

using their arms to keep branches out of their faces. Amelia followed at the rear.

They'll track us, no problem, Amelia thought. *They'll just listen for our minds.*

"Keep moving," Ty called back. "Down and to the right!"

Amelia felt, then, what he must have felt: the faintest whisper of Mara in her mind, the slightest tug in that direction.

A whoosh and then a crackling came from behind. She looked back. Fire burned in the clearing they'd just left.

Amelia thought later that it was thanks to Ty alone that they made it out alive. He seemed to know just when they should veer left or right to avoid the flares that ripped down through the treetops. He was listening for the attackers' minds, she realized, just as the attackers were listening for theirs.

They came to a place where the ground tilted. They skidded, then slid, faster and faster, into a deep cut in the mountainside. Amelia bounced over rocks and tree roots and tried to dig her heels into the muddy ground, and went on sliding. Then came two seconds in mid-air, and a series of splashes and cries of "Ow!" And they were sitting in the rocky bed of an icy stream.

Well done, Mara said.

A FEW STRIDES higher up the hill, the cut came together at the top to make the entrance to a cave. The stream flowed down from there. The cave, when they reached it, widened out farther back so there was plenty of room for Mara and her twenty dragons. Simon could see dozens of eyes gleaming at him from the darkness.

Mara crouched at the cave opening like an enormous guard dog. She stood up as they came sloshing up the stream bed.

She looked first at Ty. He stuck out his chin and tried to match her gaze, but after a couple of seconds he closed his eyes tight and sat down with a splash in the stream. Mara grinned a ferocious dragon grin and said, for all to hear: *Never fear. You have been punished enough. This time.* Creaky dragon laughter sounded from inside the cave.

Next she turned to Ammy. And Ammy, who hated getting mucky and should have been madder than a wet hen —she looked like one right now — looked up with tears on her face and then down again, as if she wasn't sure they still knew each other.

A bubble of silence formed around the two of them. Simon guessed it was something that Mara had done. Only for a minute, and then Mara lowered her giant dragon head and Ammy raised hers, and they touched.

The bubble broke. Ammy laughed joyfully. Mara glanced at Simon — a friendly nod. At Ike — a faint grin.

Last of all, she looked at John Lilac, who stood a few steps outside the cave entrance. Simon remembered that this was the brother who had tried to overthrow Mara. He had sent the Assassin to kill her and steal the ring of the Urdar chiefs, the ring she was wearing now on the thumb of her left hand.

"Brother," she said in her deep, sweet cello voice. "Do you know me?"

He hesitated, then met her eye to eye. He held the gaze a lot longer than Ty had, but at last his eyes fell. "Madam, I do not."

"Your mind is like a river choked with ice. You are no use to your people like this."

"My people?" He laughed bitterly. "I have no people."

"You have, and they are under the claw of a tyrant. I fear Zephrinarrinaden has caged their minds."

Ty leaped to his feet, changing into a dragon in the same motion and nearly knocking Simon off his feet. "He would do that? To his own people?" He looked ready to flame. "Why did you not kill him?"

"Because it was not my purpose to come here and shed blood," she said calmly.

"But he is a monster!" Hisses of agreement came from the other dragons back in the darkness of the cave.

"My purpose was to find out the truth and then help these Urdar to know the truth. Then it would be for them to decide what to do with Zeph."

"But if he has trapped their minds—"

"Only their true chief can free them." She looked at John Lilac again. "We were enemies, once. We fought. I exiled you. Will you trust me in your mind?"

He met her eyes again. "I trust nobody — least of all myself. But I do not think you desire my death. And even death were better than having this hell's brew forever in my head."

"Look at me steadily."

They stood staring into each other's eyes, not blinking, the tall dark-haired man and the big red-gold dragon. Simon's eyes started to water in sympathy. He realized he could see things better now: the sky was not so dark.

Then Mara nodded and stepped back. John Lilac took a deep breath clear to his toes, and rubbed his face with his hands. He dipped his head at Mara. "Sister, my thanks. Now I know all."

She dipped her head back at him. Nothing else happened.

Simon stared at him. "Shouldn't he be turning, um, back into a dragon?"

Mara looked at her brother and then at Ammy, as if comparing them. "So it can work the other way," she thrummed. "Remember the old story of Draum and Volund, dragon and human, the half-brothers, sons of Adam?"

"Yes." Simon remembered something else. "Pier told me the Casserine myth about how the world started. It said the same thing, pretty much."

"Maybe we are not so strange to each other as we have always thought," Mara murmured. Then she tossed her head and stretched her wings. "But now, brother, your people need a chief!"

For a moment Simon thought it wasn't going to happen. John Lilac stood with his eyes closed. Maybe he couldn't come back to what he used to be. Maybe the poisoned gate had damaged him too much. Maybe he just didn't want to.

Then he lifted his head, gave himself a shake, and transformed into a huge indigo-purple dragon with glowing lilac eyes. He was even bigger than Mara.

"Come!" he cried, in a voice like a bass viol. He sprang into the air. Mara took off right behind him, then Ammy, suddenly in dragon shape, and Ty. The others streamed after them. Simon and Ike flattened themselves against the sides of the ravine, hoping not to be trampled. Then they stood at the cave mouth watching twenty-and-some dragons melt into the pre-dawn twilight.

"So what now?" Ike shook his head at them. "Fight? They'll never win, a couple of dozen against what, a couple of hundred?"

Chiefs' talk.

They looked around. A green dragon with a pearly sheen to its scales stood behind them. It was the only one left.

They will call for a parley.

"And you stayed to tell us that?" Ike said brightly. "Well, thank—"

I am told to bring you. Climb on.

Chapter 27

Battle to the Death

THE PARLEY PLACE was a shallow, rocky bowl scooped out of the side of a hill north of the city. Now that the sky was lighter, you could see the long lines of dragons flying in from all directions and spiralling down to land.

Mara and her followers had got there first. They had taken the strongest position in the bowl. John Lilac — no, it should be Tarq, now — crouched on a big boulder that stuck out at the higher end. Mara and Ty lined up on either side of him, and the rest of Mara's dragons spread out behind them. This meant they were looking down on Zeph's dragons in the lower part of the bowl.

Good move, Simon thought, as Pearlygreen circled in to land. The position made Tarq and his group seem stronger. He hoped it would make up a little for the fact that the other dragons outnumbered them ten to one.

Pearlygreen landed near the top edge of the bowl, dumped Ike and Simon into a patch of something scratchy that smelled like lavender, and loped down to join the others. Ike and Simon climbed higher, to where boulders stuck out among the trees.

"Best seat in the house," Ike said, as he perched on a rock.

When the bowl was nearly filled with dragons, and nothing moved except the gleam of eyes, a latecomer flew in slowly from the east. He circled lazily a few times, as if to make sure nobody missed his massive size and the hard gleam of his iron-grey scales. Then he settled in the centre of the bowl. He must have seen Tarq and Mara and the others, but, deliberately, he turned his back on them and looked down at his followers.

"I have a feeling that's not how this is supposed to go," Simon said.

A thin human shape wriggled out from between two dragons. Ammy. She slouched up the slope towards them, gloomily kicking stones out of her way.

"Mara sent me back," she announced, when she was near enough. "She said, in case anything bad happens, I'm supposed to grab you two and fly to the gate."

"Good to have an escape plan," Ike said. "So when does the parley start?"

"It's started. Only, it's not a real parley. They're not talking back and forth, like they should be. Zeph's ignoring Mara and Tarq. I can tell how bad they think that is — they're just boiling inside."

"I can't hear anything," Simon said.

"It's all mind talk, and it's shielded — it's only for dragons. I can hear most of it, though." Ammy climbed up on the rock they shared and wriggled in between them. "Zeph's telling his people what a bad chief Tarq was." She tilted her head, eyes closed. "He says they all thought Tarq was dead but he wasn't — he was just a coward. He ran away to the demon world because he knew he wasn't up to the job of being chief. And look, he brought back demons with him."

Down in the bowl, necks turned and heads lifted. All eyes were fixed on the three human figures perched at the top of the bowl.

"Demons! Man!" Ike rolled his eyes.

"Shh!" She listened some more. "Zeph says, Tarq ran away, so you can't trust him. Who knows what he might do? Maybe he'll bring armies of demons with weapons of power, and kill all the dragons."

"They won't swallow that!" Simon felt cold. "Will they?"

The bowl below Zeph was a stirring mass of dragonflesh. Ike glanced across the valley towards the ledge where the gate was. "Maybe we better..."

"Wait!" Ammy said.

During Zeph's speech, Tarq had crouched silent and motionless. Now he raised his head and spat flame. The plume sizzled through the air about six inches above Zeph's head. Zeph whirled around and for the first time looked up.

"Good for Tarq!" Simon whispered.

Ammy listened intently. "Tarq says that's all .... snake poop, I think he said. Just what you'd expect from a snake. Zeph is a liar, a murderer and an oath-breaker."

Ike whistled. Simon could hear the stir from here. Clawed feet shuffled, tails flicked.

"Zeph says this is all just words." The stir went still. Ammy laughed. "What a stupid thing to say! Words are really important to dragons! Zeph knows that!"

Tarq looked down at Zeph, who sneered up at him. Then Tarq stood up on his haunches so that he towered over the valley. His huge blue-purple wings unfolded and spread wide. At that moment the sun slid over the mountain behind them and lit him up. He shone sapphire and gold.

For a moment he just stood like that. Simon thought he must be scanning the crowd, meeting all the eyes. One thing was sure, nobody was looking at anything else but Tarq. Not even Zeph.

Ammy leaned forward. "My words are truth, he says. I swear to this by my true name, Tar—" She sat back. "He's swearing an oath! Omigosh! And broadcasting his true name! Tarquinarrinadel! He says he owes it to them because they are his people. And now—" Her hands flew to her mouth. "Now he's going to open his mind and let

168

them in! All of them! He says they can read the truth of what happened for themselves."

The dragons were dead quiet. The moment stretched out.

And then all heads turned and all eyes looked at Zeph.

"Now you know me inside out, Tarq says. And if Zeph is so sure he has the truth, he will open his mind in the same way."

Zeph flared. The dragons around him shuffled away.

"Zeph says there's only one right way to settle this. By single combat. To the death."

Tarq and Zeph looked at each other. Then Tarq leaped into the air. Zeph followed.

"They're actually doing it!" Ammy sat up.

"But why would Zeph do that?" Simon stared up at the circling dragons. "Tarq's younger and probably stronger. He's sure to win."

"But Zeph's a dirty fighter, I bet," Ike said. "He's got some tricks up his sleeve."

"It's all he's got left," Ammy said. "He knows he can't give his people the truth, and they know it. All he can do is try to prove he's strongest."

LOOKING BACK LATER, Amelia knew the battle couldn't have lasted more than ten minutes. But it seemed to go on forever, the indigo and the iron-grey dragon darting and flaming high in the pale blue sky. Tarq was faster and more agile, but Zeph slammed him like a mountain falling, and his flares looked whiter and hotter.

The watching dragons sat still and silent, but their minds shouted. Waves of hope and anger and fear washed over Amelia.

The fighters broadcast nothing. Amelia wondered, then realized why. They were shielding their minds from each other.

Then came the moment when Zeph and Tarq had spun and circled out over the bay, and a flare shot out, and Tarq's scream of pain broke through his shield. The dragons on the hillside cried out with him.

"Tarq's hurt!" Amelia gasped.

"They're all tangled up." Ike squinted under his hand. "They're wrestling in mid-air."

"Now one of them's falling," Simon said. "Which one?"

A terrible cry of hatred and despair blasted through Amelia's mind and left her clutching her head. A big shape plunged to the sea.

The survivor circled once, close above the waves. Then he beat upwards and began flying slowly back.

"Who is it?" Ike was jumping up and down and about to fall off the rock. "Can you see?"

Simon had guessed. "Look at them." He nodded down at the dragons. "They know."

The dragons in the bowl were taking to the air, bugling and thrumming and fluting. First the exiles, and then Mara and Ty and their people burst up and fanned out. The sky was a wheeling dance of dragons, all colours, flashing in the morning sun.

The returning fighter was flying slower, sinking towards the ground. He was over the city now. "He needs help," Simon said.

Amelia found she had transformed without meaning to. She gripped the rock with her claws while Ike and Simon picked themselves out of the bushes on either side. Every muscle in her body tensed to fly, to join the others.

But I can't.

She let the dragon shape go. Simon climbed back onto the rock beside her. "Why not?" he said. "You want to be up there, anybody can see that. You keep pawing at the air."

She shrugged. "This is their party. I'd just be an outsider."

A skyful of dragons swirled around Tarq, bore him up, and flew him home.

Chapter 28

The Dead and Living City

"SO THINGS ARE looking up." Simon watched the dragons at the bottom of the parley place. Mara and Ty and ten of the exiles lay in a wheel pattern with them as the spokes and Tarq as the hub. The rest of the dragons had flown away.

Amelia said they were having a council meeting. "And I'm not supposed to listen."

The three had spent an hour exploring the woods above the bowl, while the sun climbed up the sky. They'd found a stream of clear water, and trees with fruit that looked like small pears but tasted like grapes.

"Funny." Ike took a moment to spit out a seed. "Look at Tarq down there. You wouldn't think he'd just won a battle to the death and saved his people from a brutal dictator."

"What d'you expect?" Amelia flicked her nibbled core at a flock of crow-like birds. "He was wounded. He's worn out. And he's just barely come unscrambled. Of course he'd be quiet."

Suddenly she stood up. Mara and Ty had unplugged themselves from the dragon wheel and came bounding up the hill.

"There will be talk for hours yet," Mara thrummed. "You three can go home."

"Are they going to be all right?" Simon asked. "I mean, did Zeph hurt their minds?"

"Some were hurt. Most were only fooled. Dragons can be stupid,

171

too." Her eyes gleamed bright green with amusement. "I can help with the healing. But not too much, for they are proud."

"Are you going to let them come home again?" Ammy asked.

"I have said I will welcome any who will swear loyalty to me. But I think none will. They have their own homeland now and their own chief. They will do well here."

"Only, not *here*." Ty looked over his shoulder at the city.

"No, not here. This place will never be safe."

They all turned to look at the city spread below. It was beautiful, Simon thought. It shone in the sun, white and lush green. It didn't look dangerous.

"My kinsman, here, tells me about your troubles," Mara said. "I have never heard of such a thing before, a sick gate." She stretched her wings. "We will go and look."

THE CLOSER they came to the city, the more it looked like a ruin. Most of the buildings were heaps of tumbled stone with trees growing in and around them. Only a few white towers were whole.

They landed in the centre of the city, in a long, wide, open patch that led up, like an avenue, to the tallest tower.

Mara transformed as soon as her feet touched down. She wore the jeans and red-sequined jacket Ammy had given her last winter. Simon guessed this was the easiest shape for her to take. It was the human version of her as a dragon: emerald-eyed, tall, proud, with a mane of red-gold hair.

Ty shaped the boy with spiked blue-green hair they'd seen before. Ammy-dragon looked at Mara in her shining coat, squeezed her eyes shut, and took half a minute to change. When she finished, she looked down at herself and sighed. She wore the same stained, ripped jeans and hoodie she'd been wearing before.

"I was trying to shape a new leather jacket," she said glumly.

"With diamond studs."

Mara smiled at her. "That too will come. You are stronger each time I see you. But now, hurry." She glanced up the avenue at the tall white tower. "We must not stay long. There is a kind of death here."

They walked on. The tower rose higher above them. When they reached its base they had to crane their necks to see the top. The building looked to be made of snow-white china. Its corners looked razor-sharp and as smooth as if they'd been cut yesterday.

The entrance was a tall, wide opening that led into a maze of halls and corridors, all made of the same flawless white stone. A radiant band near the ceiling soaked all the stone with a soft glow.

Ty hesitated at the top of a ramp. "Down here, I think." The ramp led down to a level with lower ceilings and dimmer light. They walked along narrow corridors broken by the outlines of small doors set flush into the walls. There were no handles.

One of the doors stood open. Simon cautiously poked his head inside. No glowing walls here. It was just a dark, bare room about six feet long and three feet wide. He wondered if all these doors led to empty closets, and why.

At the end of the corridor they walked into an enormous room. It was so high that the ceiling was lost in a creamy glow. The opposite wall looked a mile off. The gigantic space was filled with hundreds of narrow tables, each about the size of a human adult.

Simon looked at them uneasily. They reminded him of something, he wasn't sure what.

"There it is." Ty pointed. "There is the gate."

The door was set in the centre of the far wall. From here it looked like all the other doors in this place. You only knew it was there because of an outline in the stone.

"Come, then." Mara set off briskly towards it and the others followed, filing between the tables. They walked directly towards the

173

door. Simon kept wanting to look away from it. But every time he looked back at it, it seemed to have grown larger. He began to dread looking up.

Ammy walked with her hands in her hoodie pocket, shoulders hunched. "What kind of a place is this?"

"It looks like a hospital," Ike said.

Ty shook his head. "I remember the hospital in Dunstone, the place of healing. There was pain and fear there, but also hope. Here, there is no hope."

"Not a hospital." Simon suddenly knew what it reminded him of. "A lab." Those tables, each just big enough for one person. His heart pattered. He walked faster.

"Funny!" Ike had on his too-bright face. "Like brings like, remember? If that gate connects to the one at our end, this place oughta be more like a mall. Or a school. Or, or..."

"Or a jail," Simon said. "Maybe it is. All those little rooms back there."

"Never mind, we'll be out of here in no time." Ike trotted to catch up to Mara, who was striding ahead.

They stepped out from among the tables and Simon inhaled a lungful of relief. Then he looked up at the door. It was only three dragon paces away now.

This close, you could see that it was about ten feet high and five feet wide. Just an outline, no handle, no frame. Nothing showed on its white surface except for their dim reflections.

"Are we sure this is a world gate?" Ike started forward.

Ty grabbed him by the shoulder. "Do not touch it!"

"Of course it is a gate." Mara studied it. "Can you not feel?"

"I do." Amelia edged up against Ty. "It's alive. I can hear it. Only, it... it doesn't sing like the others."

"It is calling." Mara looked at Simon. "It wants you."

174

Simon's hands shook. He made fists, took a couple of steadying breaths, and walked towards the gate.

"Don't go near!" Ty shouted.

"I just need to see something."

He stopped about three feet away and stared at the shiny surface. There was his shadowy reflection, with Ammy's at his shoulder — he was surprised to find her there — and the others smaller, farther back behind him. Nothing else. No DAWG T-shirt, no hillside, no stars.

"Okay, let's go." He took a step back, unwilling to turn his back on the gate.

The reflections vanished. Other images formed, as if rising out of a pool of milk: a sloping line, a climbing figure, a reaching hand.

The door's white shine darkened to the colour of mud.

Ammy pulled at his jacket. "Get back!"

The surface bulged forward. It reached for Simon.

Chapter 29

Lost in Transit

SIMON FROZE. He watched the bubble of darkness bulge closer.

Simon, came the voice. *Simon. Please.*

Sharp-pointed hands grabbed him under the arms. The floor dropped from under his feet and he spun around and sailed across the room. The tables flicked under his dangling feet.

Amelia dropped Simon at the front of the room, near the entrance. Mara, and Ty carrying Ike, sank down beside them. Then they all ran, and they didn't stop running until they were out of the building and under the open sky.

AMELIA DIDN'T even slow down until she was well away from the tower. Then she curled her neck back to look at it. "How could anyone make something as horrible as that?"

"Ardini can," Mara said coolly. "Whatever happened there happened many ages ago, yet the stink of it has not faded. It must have been very bad."

"That explains why the place at our end is the way it is," Ike said. "Like brings like."

Simon walked around in front of Mara. "Can't you do something about it?"

"Of course. My brother's people can keep a watch on this place from a safe distance, and spread the word to avoid it."

"That's fine for the dragons, they can just fly away! But in

Dunstone they can't do that! And there are three thousand people living close to that gate!"

"Then you must break the gate," Mara said gently.

"Break it!" Simon stared. "How?"

"I do not know," Mara thrummed. "This is not a thing for dragons. We can bury gates, but not break them. Humans made the gates, and only humans can destroy them. It is for you, children of Wayland."

"Well, Pier could do it," Amelia said. "So I should be able to."

"But suppose we go into that gate and come out like Ty and John Lilac?" Ike shook his head. "With our minds wiped? No way!"

"Maybe if we just clean out that cell," Simon said. "Maybe if we take out Jacob's bones and get them properly buried. That might make things a bit better. At least it's something we can do."

Because we have to do something. The thought hung in the air between them.

With Ike riding on Ty and Simon on Amelia, they lifted off and flew to the black stone ledge with the row of three gates. Everything after that was a little too brisk, Amelia thought. Mara brushed her mind with a smile, then said aloud: "You may see me again. Someday." She sprang into the air and dwindled to a knife-shape carving the sky above the valley.

Amelia stared after her. *May see me again? And that means what, exactly?*

When she looked around, Ty had set Simon down and taken human shape again: jeans, DAWG T-shirt, hoodie. She transformed too.

"I must go now," Ty said. "I will speak with this other chief, my father. Maybe he will let me stay here and explore. Who knows what new lands lie over there, beyond those hills?" He waved at the eastern horizon.

177

Oh, if only I could stay too! If only I could go flying off into the sunset with you!

It would be the sunrise, not the sunset. But why can't you?

I can't. Not yet, not right now. I can't just go off and leave my parents.

You honour your kin. That is good.

Ty suddenly pulled off the hoodie and the red DAWG T-shirt. He dropped the hoodie on the ground. Then he looked at Amelia. "Take this, ardin child." He pushed the wad of red cotton into her hands. "This will give you something of me while you are far away. And maybe we will meet again."

And then he was Ty-dragon again, and then he was aloft, and then he was gone.

Amelia walked towards the brink of the ledge so Simon and Ike couldn't look at her. She blotted her wet face with the DAWG T-shirt. It was still warm and it smelled like him, like cinnamon and sulphur and honey.

When she turned around, Simon was frowning at the T-shirt. "We just can't get rid of that thing, can we?" he said.

She rolled the shirt up and stuck it under her arm. "Let's get home."

THE FIRST PASSAGE spilled them out onto the ledge on the other side of the ocean. Here on Mara's side of the world it was night.

"Kind of a jolt." Ike blinked. "So bright on the other side. I wonder..."

"If that made the passage seem dark? Don't think so." Simon rubbed his arms, wishing he could rub off what he'd felt in the passage. Shadowy, half-solid things slithering over him, pawing at him.

"Funny." Amelia was shaping the dragon as she spoke. "You

178

don't think the one sick gate could make the others sick too, could it? I mean, it's not like they're people. They don't catch colds."

"Don't have to be people," Ike said cheerfully. "Computers catch viruses. There's obviously some kind of network—"

"Climb up and let's go!" Ammy bugled, and for once Simon didn't mind how pushy she was getting. His heart thumped. Time was running short. They had to get through that second passage now, this minute.

Suppose we stick in there. Suppose we never get out!

He shook that thought out of his head. He and Ike got a grip on Ammy's armoured shoulders and they flew south beneath the unfamiliar stars. Ammy followed the white frill of surf that trimmed the rocky coast.

She must have been really pounding the air, or maybe they had a good following wind. It seemed like only minutes before she banked right, soared high over a range of hills, and dipped down over what Simon thought of as Pier's valley.

The stream glimmered below. An inky shape moved on the broken mountainside. Shinyblack blinked up at them. Ammy waggled a wing at him. Twice she circled what looked to Simon like a few yards of empty air, swerving around so fast and tight he nearly lost his grip. Second time around, the tall sapphire gate formed ahead of them.

Simon laughed with relief. "It looks all right!"

Ammy circled one more time, folded her wings and dove into the opening passage.

LIGHT AND SINGING. That was what Simon always remembered from the gates. Light as blue as a clear twilight sky. Brilliant sparks zipping around. And a high silvery sound all on one pure note. As if the stars were singing.

179

Different this time. The blue light darkened and thickened. It clung like mud. The singing changed to an electric whine, and then to a thin scream. He couldn't feel his body but he could feel things tangling around him, choking him, pulling him back.

AMELIA BURST out into cold night air. October wind slapped her in the face. The Dunn River roared a few yards below. A scream of triumph and relief broke from her jaws. "We made it!" She just barely stopped herself from flaming.

Ike was shouting something. He had to shout several times before she caught it. "Simon!"

"What about Simon?"

"He's not here!"

Chapter 30

Boiling Over

"NOT THERE? But he has to be!" Amelia turned her head around on the end of its long neck. Simon wasn't on her back.

"He's stuck in the passage!" Ike shouted. "What are we going to do?"

"I don't know!" She circled around the invisible gate. She could feel its dull vibrations.

"Mara said something in there wanted him!" Ike thumped his fist on Amelia's shoulder. "Maybe it got him! We gotta do something!"

"What, go in after him?"

"Got no choice!"

Amelia didn't need to be told. She flicked a wing at the hidden gate. Nothing happened, and she remembered: she needed to touch it with something from Mythrin. Simon had the Mythrin stone. All she had was ... a wad of red cotton T-shirt. Something of me, Ty said.

Worth a try.

Next time around, she dabbed the T-shirt at the gate. It flared to life, dissolved into the passage — and Simon tipped out of it. He fell like a starfish, all spread out. Amelia dove and caught him just as he hit the water. Dangling and dripping, they climbed the air up into the sheltering night sky.

AS AMMY flapped up past the Dunning Street bridge, with Simon hanging like a scrap of wet laundry from her claws, he had a glimpse of upturned faces gaping at them. He hoped it was nobody who knew him.

Ammy settled down on the roof of the bookstore a minute later, after dropping Simon on his feet. She shrugged Ike off. Simon caught his balance, staggered to the parapet, and looked down. "Uh-oh."

The parents were crowded around the mall's front doors and were thumping on them with fists and boots. Lisa Nader and Bob Lebrun were yelling and pushing at them, trying to make them stand back.

"They got that tire iron away from Kevin's dad, anyway," Ike said.

Something moved on the flat roof of the mall above the doors. A second later, something crashed and bounced on the cement sidewalk a few inches from Lisa's foot. She looked up and pointed. More objects whizzed into the crowd. Parents yelled and covered their heads.

"Pop cans!" said Ammy, after a squint. "They're throwing cans of pop from the roof. I think I see Kevin up there."

"Wait 'til he gets home! Is he ever in for it!" Ike laughed.

One of the parents — it looked like Kevin's dad again — broke from the crowd and ran across the intersection. He got into a pickup truck that was parked on King Street, started the engine, and burst from the curb with a squeal of rubber. He screeched to a stop halfway across the intersection, with the car pointed at the mall's front doors. The horn blared. The engine gunned.

"I don't believe it!" Simon's stomach hurt. He pushed back from the parapet.

"He's going to ram the doors!" Ike was hanging nearly halfway over. "Look, the other parents are scattering! The cops are hanging on the truck windows! Lisa's trying to talk him down!"

"This is just like in the mall this afternoon." Simon pulled Ike back by his collar. "It's not funny any more. People are going crazy! It's the gate that's doing it!"

"There's no way we can do anything about that gate."

"We've got to try! We'll go in and get Jacob's bones and bring them out. Maybe that'll cool things off."

"Only one way in," Ammy said in her deep dragon voice. "The crevice in the gorge under the Queen Street bridge. And don't even think of trying to get there on foot, in the dark. We're flying!"

IT COULD have been worse, Amelia thought, fifteen minutes later. She'd taken back her human form outside the cave, then pulled on the DAWG T-shirt over her hoodie. Even with the extra shirt she was less bulky than last time, when she'd had on a leather jacket.

Ike, who came third, did okay, but Simon almost didn't make it. About halfway along he had to slide out of his jacket, and then wriggle out of his sweater, and drag them after him as he squirmed sideways past the tight places.

It was the C-shaped part at the inner end of the crevice that got him. Amelia, who had squeezed through first, coached him on breathing out and making himself as thin as possible. He still stuck.

"Can't … get … air," he rattled.

"You don't want air! You want to breathe out!"

"Got … nothing … to … breathe …"

"Ike! When I give the word, you push! When I count to three!" She gripped Simon's wrist with both hands, braced her feet, closed her eyes and thought: *dragon strength.* "Ready? One — two — three!" She leaned back and yanked with all her might.

Simon yelled and fell out of the crack, right on top of her. Before they could pick themselves up, Ike fell out on top of Simon.

When they sorted themselves out, they found Simon had left behind half of his T-shirt. The bare right half of his chest was scraped

183

and bleeding. "And my shoulder!" He shrugged it around, and winced. "I hope it's not dislocated."

"Never mind, you're out. So far, so good." She helped him put his sweater and jacket back on. "Now, where's this room with the bones?"

Ike moved the flashlight beam around. It dimmed, then brightened again. He muttered something about batteries. "It'll be okay. This way."

They walked fast, ducking their heads at the low places. More than ever, this stony maze felt to Amelia like a jail. The narrow passages and low ceilings and bricked-up side passages were like squeezing hands. When they found the bent passage with the iron door at the end, it looked like biting teeth.

She squinted at it. "I don't see any picture of Simon."

"It's there." Simon grabbed her arm and pulled her away from the door. "Keep as far away from that as you can. I don't want to set it off."

Ike nudged it open. It swung noiselessly. They crowded together in the front part of the cell, where it was high enough to stand upright. Ike shone the light on a little heap of what looked like sticks and rags in the back corner. Amelia pointed. "That stuff? That's Jacob Redding's … bones?"

"That's them," Simon said.

For a moment they just stood looking at the pitiful pile. Amelia thought: Can't be. That can't be what's left of a real, live kid. Then she looked closer, and there was no mistake.

"Dumb!" Ike whacked himself on the forehead. "We got nothing to carry them in!"

Amelia looked around for a box or something, but there was nothing else in the cell. "We could use your jacket."

"Or Simon's."

"Or that DAWG T-shirt," Simon said. "It's extra, you don't need it."

"Ty gave it to me," she began. "I don't want to—"

They hadn't been listening to anything but themselves, or they might have heard a step. But all they heard was a clang as the iron door slammed behind them. Then a second, smaller clang.

And then a squeaky laugh. "Welcome, children!" squealed a gleeful voice. "Welcome to Buckingham Palace! Enjoy your stay!"

Chapter 31

Buckingham Palace

"HEY!" Amelia yelled. "Let us out!"

Ike pounded on the door. "You can't do this!"

"I just did! This is what happens to trespassers!"

"It's the Ratman," Simon muttered. He raised his voice. "Um, Mr. Ralston? You gotta let us out! You'll get in trouble if you don't!"

"You've got it backwards, boy." The Ratman giggled. "*You're* in trouble! That's what the Palace is for. Punishing troublemakers."

"Like Jacob Redding?"

A cackle of laughter on the other side of the door. "Somebody's been doing his homework! You're right, Redding was a troublemaker. Always trying to run away."

"How do you know that?" Amelia put in. She thought she knew what Simon was trying to do. Keep the Ratman talking, maybe talk him into letting them go.

"My father told me, of course. And his father told him. My granddad that was, old Yancy. My family has a long connection with this place, beginning with my great-granddad, Cornelius." He sounded proud. You could just see him puffing out his puny chest.

"Yancy, um, he worked in the school, didn't he? Was he the one who, who put Jacob in here?"

"Of course he was. Just doing his duty. And now I'm doing mine!"

"But the thing is," said Simon in his most patient and reasonable

186

tone. "The thing is, that's history. They do things differently now. You can't leave us in here. You see that, right?"

No answer.

"Mr. Ralston?" Amelia called. "Please! Please let us out!" She thought she heard a high-pitched laugh off in the distance. Then nothing. "He's gone. He's left us. Just like Jacob."

"Well, we're not going to end up like Jacob!" Ike handed her the flashlight. "C'mon, Simon, let's break the door down!"

"I'm not touching it!"

"Okay, then." Ike turned sideways, braced himself, and rammed his left shoulder against the door. "Ow!" He bounced off and collapsed against the wall, clutching his shoulder.

Amelia tried next. *Dragon strength!* No good: the door held firm. She backed away from it and brushed at rusty brown marks on the DAWG T-shirt. She still couldn't see any picture of Simon on the scabby surface. "What are we going to do?"

"Well, we're not going to be stuck in here forever, don't worry." Simon, who had the flashlight now, shone it around. It flickered over the bones in the back corner. "Sooner or later, Harry'll realize he has to let us out. All we have to do is wait."

"You think?" Ike rubbed his shoulder.

"I mean, he can't be completely crazy."

Nobody said anything.

They sat down in a row under the sloping roof, facing the door, with Simon in the middle. Amelia thought of Jacob Redding.

Simon must have been thinking of him too. "Imagine if you were shut up here without a light," he said. "It would be black as tar."

"Blacker," Ike said.

"And no sound." Amelia hugged herself and shivered. "And it would be cold. And damp." She grimaced at the green-stained cracks in the ceiling.

"I just can't believe anybody would…" The light wavered again and went out. Simon made a sound of disgust. "Ike!"

"I forgot! I'm sorry!"

Simon clinked the flashlight on the floor, but it stayed dead. Amelia reached for his hand. It was shaking. She didn't blame him. Even with dragon sight, she could barely make out the shape of the door a couple of feet away. For him and Ike, it must be as if something had stolen the world.

It must have been like that for Jacob too. Only worse, much worse, because he'd been alone. Her mind flinched away from the thought.

And then, deliberately, she pulled the thought back. Jacob, a boy about their age. All alone. Curled up to try and stay warm. Day after day, until there was no day, no night. Only the darkness and the silence and the cold.

Jacob, finally understanding that he would never again see the light. Never see his parents. That he would die alone in the dark because nobody cared enough to come and get him.

Tears trickled down her cheeks and onto her hands. Beside her, Simon took a shaky breath. "This is what really poisoned this end of the gate," he said. "It was bad enough to start with. That awful place on the other side. The jail and the school on this side. All the hatred and fear and misery. But then Jacob died in here. That's what really did it."

Ike said: "I don't think anything we can do with his bones will ever fix that."

"Maybe. But we have to try."

"When we get out—" Amelia stared hard at the door. It was easier and easier for her to see. She thought something on it had moved. "Can you see anything?"

"Not a thing," Ike growled.

188

"Me neither," Simon said. "But wait—" His voice brightened. "I've still got the Mythrin stone. If I hold it I can see… uh … "

"Can you see the door?" Ike said. "What's happening?"

"I th-think…" Simon cleared his throat. "The — the gate. It's starting to open."

THE GATE took shape. All by itself: nobody had touched it. Mind of its own, Simon thought, and wished he hadn't.

With the Mythrin stone tight in his fist he could see it clearly. The iron door with the image of him climbing had sunk back into a slab of darkly glistening mud. That's what it looked like: greenish-brownish-greyish mud, with dead weeds twisting through it. With a dim glow coming off it, like a light behind a scummy window.

Worse than this afternoon — had it only been this afternoon?

"Stay back," he said, not taking his eyes off the gate.

Ammy put her hand on his arm. "You too." He had got up onto his knees.

That voice again, soft and distant. *Simon.*

"You hear that?"

"Hear what?"

Simon! Clearer now: a boy's voice.

"Who are you?" But he guessed. He shuffled forward on his knees. "What do you want?"

The gate opened. The sick glow faded. The passage burrowed into darkness.

"No!" Ammy dug her fingers into his sleeve. "Don't go in there!"

"'Course not." He rose to a crouch. He took a step forward, half unwilling.

Simon, help! Please help!

"I think I know who's calling."

"It could be a trap!" Ike yelled in his ear. "Don't take the

189

chance!"

Don't take the chance? Right, Simon thought. And never know. Always be wondering, for the rest of your life. Wondering if you'd left him alone in the dark, forever.

Simon got a good grip on the Mythrin stone, for courage. He stepped into the passage.

Chapter 32

Shadow Land

"WHAT ARE YOU doing here?"

Amelia jumped. She hadn't noticed Simon standing behind her. "Same thing you are, I guess. I tried to hold you back, but I got pulled in too."

"I wasn't pulled. I went."

"What the heck for?"

"For Jacob. In case it really is him in here."

"And you're supposed to be the cautious one! Where's Ike?"

Simon looked around. "He must have let go before he got pulled in."

"He's the smart one," Amelia said. "All right, where are we?"

There was almost nothing to see. They seemed to be standing in a narrow street, and it seemed to be night. "Seemed," because Amelia wasn't sure.

If there was sky above, she couldn't see it. The ground under her shoes felt like cement. Tall buildings ran along both sides. Doorways and windows opened into darkness.

"This is about the deadest place I've ever seen," Amelia said. No lights, no people, no birds, not a single stray cat. No grass, no trees. No breeze. The air smelled of nothing at all.

And there was no colour. Even the red DAWG T-shirt looked black.

"I don't hear the voice any more." Simon tilted his head. "Well, no point staying here." He started off along the street. She kept pace with him.

"Wherever this is, I don't think it's Mythrin." Amelia sauntered, hands in pockets, to show how unafraid she was. "This makes me think of that in-between place I was in, last year, with Mara. She called it—"

Simon grabbed her wrist. He stared at the nearest window. "Something moved in there."

She peered. He was right. Something stirred in the blackness and moved towards them. They backed away. Then walked on, faster, shoulder to shoulder. They kept to the centre of the road, which began to climb.

Something caught the corner of Amelia's eye. When she looked back, a man was following them along the street a few paces back. "Simon!" He turned and they grabbed hands.

The man didn't even look at them. He turned into a doorway. Darkness swallowed him. He had been completely ordinary-looking, except for his feet. They were birds' claws.

Simon let out the breath he'd been holding. "So it's not so dead. There are people."

"That was a person?"

A few doors and windows later they walked out into an open square. It was so big and dark that they could only just see the buildings on the far side. Something stuck up in the middle, which Amelia guessed, after squinting at it through the murk, was a fountain with a wide basin and a statue on a pedestal.

There were many more people here. Shadowy figures drifted across the square. Simon and Amelia walked slowly through the throng, careful not to bump into anyone.

"Nobody even looks at us," Amelia muttered. "What's wrong with them?"

"They don't look at each other, either. They don't speak."

"Well, I'm going to get someone to tell me what this place is. I'll ask her." Simon hissed at her to stop, but Amelia took two steps towards a slim, young-looking woman walking past. Her clothes were a long, silky, pale tunic and loose pants. Dark hair waved around a lovely face. *She looks nice. I wonder how she got here?*

"Excuse me?" Amelia touched the woman's silken arm. The woman turned her head. Her eyes floated forward on stalks. Snail's eyes.

Amelia jumped back with her heart thudding. "I don't think they're really alive," she whispered. "They can't be." The woman melted into the clotted darkness.

"No dragons, you notice?" Simon murmured. "They're all human."

"Well, sort of."

A *sort of* humanity was all these people had in common. There was a man who could have come from a photo in that book about the Dunstone Gaol. He strutted along in a uniform with a long belted jacket, a sword, and a peaked cap. Others might have been prisoners, judging by their shapeless grey clothing and hopeless faces. One was a schoolteacher: he carried a long wooden pointer like Mrs. Bloomer's. There were boys, too, all dressed alike in grey sweaters and black pants.

Other people wore silky tunics or flowing robes. They didn't look as if they could ever have lived in Dunstone. Amelia nudged Simon, and pointed. He nodded. "Mythrin people."

Many of them were only part human, like the man with bird's feet and the woman with snail's eyes. One man had skin that shone like aluminum foil. One woman had fluttering gills on her neck and fins on her arms.

One man scurried bent over, with his head below his hunched

shoulders. Amelia got only glimpses of him darting among the walkers. He made her think of the Ratman.

"Funny how they never bump into each other," Amelia muttered to Simon. They moved as if they were all part of a huge, slow dance, and each one knew the steps by heart. Like they'd been doing it forever. She stared at face after face. Nobody looked back at her. "Who are all these people? How did they get in here?"

"Here's what I think." Simon looked around glumly. "They're all people who lived too close to that gate. People who died and got sucked in. Both ends."

They reached the fountain in the middle of the square. Amelia was not surprised to find it dry. She frowned up at the winged statue that stood on a pedestal in the centre of the basin. "Who at the Mythrin end?"

"Remember that room under the tower? With all the tables? I thought it might be a lab."

"You think ...." She broke off to stare at a man with an extra set of arms growing from his shoulders.

"I think somebody experimented on their own people. They made monsters. And Mara's right! It was so bad, it still stinks."

"And at the Dunstone end ... people in the jail, and the training school."

"Yes, people like—" Simon caught his breath, then lifted a finger to point. "Like him."

Chapter 33

Jacob Climbs

A BOY SAT on the curb of the fountain on the far side, with his feet in the dry basin. He was thin and small, with a mop of ragged dark hair hanging over his face. He was wearing only some sort of thin shorts, like underwear. His arms were white sticks.

"Jacob," Simon said quietly, across the dry fountain. "Jacob Redding."

The boy looked up, and, yes, it was the face in Mr. Manning's book. He shaped an *oh!* and jumped up and ran across the basin. He vaulted over the curb and landed with a slap of bare feet in front of them.

"It's you! I knew you'd come!" His dark eyes moved from Ammy's face to Simon's. "It... it is you, isn't it?" He looked uncertain now. "You've come to take me home?"

"You bet!" Simon said, much more confidently than he felt. "So it was you who was calling me?"

"Yes, that was me." Jacob's eyes shone. "You heard me!"

"And it was you who made the starry window? How did you do that?"

"Starry window?" Jacob looked confused.

"You didn't? But if it wasn't you ..." Simon frowned. *Who else in here...*

"How did you know we were coming?" Ammy asked.

"Don't know. I just knew. Something told me. Something

showed me your faces." He grabbed Ammy's hand and clung to it for a moment. "It was a long time. I got so lonely. But I never stopped hoping."

He looked at them expectantly. Ammy poked Simon. "Let's go, then!"

"Uh, yeah. Let's—" Simon looked around, and his spine chilled. Ammy looked where he was looking. She flinched.

The people in the square were standing still. Every one of them had turned to stare at him and Ammy and Jacob with their empty eyes.

Ammy cleared her throat. "Which way?" she whispered.

"Back the way we came looks good to me right now," Simon whispered.

Ammy took Jacob's hand and they walked stiffly back through the silent crowd. Faces turned and eyes tracked them as they passed. They came to the gap in the buildings where the road they'd come in by joined the square. Simon took two steps down the slope and stopped.

A moving darkness filled the far end of the street. It gurgled towards them, swallowing up pavement and doors and windows.

"What *is* that? Water? Mud?" Ammy bent towards it. Jacob tugged at her hand.

They backed up into the square. The people still stood there watching. Simon looked around. "There's another entrance over there." He pointed across the square.

"There's four." Jacob spoke up. "One on each side."

"One of them's got to be the way home." Ammy swung Jacob's hand and smiled at him. He tried to smile back but didn't quite make it.

They walked clockwise around the outside of the square. The next road also led downward. A dozen paces down its length, the liquid darkness inched towards them.

The third road was the same, only the flood was nearer.

One road left to try. When they stood at the entrance, Simon's hopes lifted. This road was different from the other three. It led upward, not down. Up into deep, velvety darkness. That was bad. But there was no hint of the water, mud, whatever it was, up there. That was good.

"Where does this road go?" Ammy asked.

Jacob shook his head. "I've no notion."

"But hasn't anybody ever tried walking out of here?"

"I don't think so." Jacob scratched his head. "Don't think anybody has tried anything at all. People don't do much of anything here. It gets very boring."

Simon thought of something that jolted him. "Um, Jacob? You do know you're, um ..." *dead?* He couldn't make himself say it. He decided that if Jacob didn't know, he wasn't going to tell him.

"You know where this place is?" Ammy asked quickly.

"No. I just know I don't belong here. None of us do." Jacob smiled, a better try than last time. "That's why you're here, right? You were sent. Like angels. To rescue us all."

Rescue us all. Like angels. Simon exchanged a horrified look with Ammy. Then looked back across the square. The aimless crowd was drifting in this direction now, like iron filings after a magnet. *And we're the magnet.*

At three places around the outside of the square, dark water was trickling in. Time to go.

They held hands, with Jacob in the middle, and climbed. The square shapes of doors and windows faded into the darkness. It grew colder. The ground became rough. Vague, bulgy shapes stuck out of the dimness.

"I don't think we're in a town any more," Simon said. "I think we're climbing a hill."

"I think we're climbing a mountain!" Ammy puffed. "My knees are killing me. And it's so darn cold!"

Jacob didn't complain, although he was barefoot and wearing next to nothing. "I wonder if I have a baby brother or sister by now?" he said suddenly. "I wonder if my dad got work? It's hard to get news of home at the school."

They climbed and climbed. It grew colder. When Simon looked back, he saw a dim crowd climbing the hillside below them. Something scurried and sneaked among them.

Farther down the long slope, a liquid darkness gleamed.

"That water." Ammy pointed. "It's coming after us!"

"All we have to do is stay ahead."

"What if we get to a place where we can't go on? What if it catches up to us?"

Simon quickened his step.

"Funny thing," Ammy said. "When I look back I keep thinking I see the Ratman."

"Me too."

"But he can't be here, can he? He's not dead."

"That's what I thought. But suppose—"

"Hey, look!" Ammy stabbed a finger upward. "There's light up there!"

"Light?" Simon tilted his head way back. It was true. Golden pinpoints gleamed overhead.

"Stars!" Ammy let go of Jacob's hand and spread her arms wide. "Stars!" she laughed.

"If they really are stars," Simon said.

"Of course they are! That means we're in the real world again! We're out!"

"Don't count on it," he said, but she wasn't listening.

"Stars?" Jacob stared at Ammy's joyful face. Then he looked up. His mouth fell open. "Stars!" he breathed.

A rustling sound came from down the hill, faint as one leaf brushing another. The shadowy people had stopped climbing and were looking up. First the nearest, then the ones farther back, more and more pale ovals tilting up.

A murmur rose, so soft Simon wasn't sure he heard it. *The stars — the stars!*

"It's like it's the first time they've seen the stars in years," Ammy said.

"More like thousands of years, for some." Simon nudged Jacob on the shoulder. "Jacob? Weren't there stars here before?"

"I don't know." Jacob couldn't take his eyes off the sky. "If there were, nobody knew. Nobody ever looked up. Not 'til you came."

Perhaps because of the stars, or perhaps because things were changing in this changeless land, there was more light. Enough to show that they were, as Ammy had guessed, climbing a mountainside. Not far ahead, another few minutes of climbing, it rose to a ridge, black on the gold-flecked sky beyond. A small peak stuck up from the ridge.

"We'll go around that knob," Simon said. "Maybe the way out will be on the other side."

"I don't know if Jacob can make it," Amelia muttered back.

Jacob still stood gazing at the stars. He had wrapped his thin arms around his bony chest. He was quivering like a guitar string.

"And look." Ammy pointed at the ground. There was light enough now to see dark smudges on the stones around his feet. "Jacob!" She knelt down. "Your feet are bleeding! Why didn't you tell us?"

He blinked down at her. "It's nothing. I've been worse off."

Simon sat down on the ground and pulled off his sneakers.

Ammy helped him work the shoes onto Jacob's feet. It wasn't easy, because Jacob kept shuffling backwards and protesting. "I can't take your shoes! You need them!"

"Nope. Look, I have socks." Simon stuck out a foot to show his good, thick, tight-knit, real wool socks.

The sneakers were a couple of sizes too big for Jacob, but Simon laced them up tight. That would have to do.

Jacob was still freezing, though. Simon stood up and started to shrug off his jacket. "You can have my sweater," he said.

And then stopped, an arm in one sleeve and the other sleeve dangling. He looked at Jacob, who was turning his feet to admire the gleaming stars on his ankles. He looked at Ammy. She looked down at herself. She looked at Jacob.

"Uh-*huh*," she said.

When she pulled the DAWG T-shirt over her head and handed it to Jacob, he protested again. "Look, I have layers underneath," she said cheerfully. "You need it, take it!"

So Jacob pulled on the T-shirt. He smoothed the loose folds down over his stomach. It didn't seem like much, but he stopped shivering. When they set out again, he took the lead.

Ammy looked up at the climbing figure a few feet above them. "He's your starry window come to life," she whispered to Simon. "He even looks a bit like you. The hair, anyway."

"I hope we're doing the right thing," he whispered back.

"It's meant! It has to be. We never planned this."

"No. Something else planned it. That's what worries me."

They kept climbing, and the shadowy people climbed silently behind them. Jacob reached the crest first. He stood at the base of the small pinnacle, looking down. His face went blank.

"Uh-oh!" Ammy scrambled after him. Simon followed.

The three of them stood on the crest together. There was no other side. They stood on the brink of a cliff that dropped sheer into a sea of darkness.

Simon glanced back. The muddy flood crawled nearer. It was just a few paces behind the last of the climbers.

So this is the end. Then he looked up, and saw something that lifted his heart. "Look!" He pointed at the pinnacle. It reached about twelve feet above their heads. "Up there!"

"That? What good will that do?" Ammy scowled up at the peak. Then she scowled at the sky behind it. "Now, that's weird."

"The stars." Simon couldn't help feeling smug. "I said they might not be, didn't I?"

The stars looked much nearer, ragged splotches of yellow light that didn't glitter.

"Not stars?" Jacob's mouth drooped.

"No, they're something better." Simon groped at the pinnacle, found handholds and footholds, and started climbing. Over his shoulder he added, "They're holes!"

He let them work that out. It meant they had come to a wall. And there were holes in the wall. And there was light on the other side.

"What are you going to do?" Ammy called.

"Try and see through!" He was at the very top now. There was just room up here for two or three people to stand.

He looked down. The dark sea was a little nearer. He looked up, and from here the holes in the sky looked to be just beyond his reach. He bent his knees and jumped straight up, arms stretched and fingers crooked.

"Careful!" Ammy and Jacob shouted, one over the other. Simon landed, staggered, caught his balance.

Missed! But by how much? A couple of inches? A yard? Ten yards?

Simon was flexing his knees to leap a second time when Ammy

yelled, "Watch out!" Right on top of the words a weight landed on his shoulders and dug its claws in.

"Vandals!" it shrieked. Bristly whiskers scraped his ear. Long yellow teeth scissored next to his cheek. Simon lunged and twisted, trying to shake the thing off. It clung like Velcro.

"Miscreants!" it squealed. "Law-breakers! Trespassers! Crim— "

Simon suddenly bent double. The creature flipped off his shoulders and whirled snout over tail off the cliff. Simon lurched, took a step, and stepped on nothing.

Ammy screamed.

The last thing Simon saw was the Ratman, now much more rat than man, dropping nose-first into the black sea. It swallowed him up, tail and all.

The darkness swirled up at Simon. He closed his eyes tight.

Chapter 34

To Pluck a Star

SIMON FELL like a toppled windmill. Amelia grabbed one flailing hand and hung on. His weight pulled her down flat on the edge of the cliff, then pulled her forward until she was half over the edge. She stared down past Simon's head into the rising black sea. It didn't look like water. It looked thick and powerful, like blood. She slid some more.

That all happened within two racing heartbeats. On the third beat, hands grabbed her ankles and hauled her back. Jacob, she thought, although she was surprised he'd have the strength.

Other hands clamped on her knees. Other arms reached down past hers. Hands locked onto Simon's wrists. Two more thumps of the heart, and Simon was up beside her on the ridge. He melted into a heap.

"Thank you! Oh, thank you!" Amelia babbled.

The man with two pairs of arms stood up and backed away. Other dark shapes drifted back into the crowd of shadow-people down the hill.

"They all wanted to help," Jacob said. "There wasn't room." He helped Simon sit up.

Simon took three or four giant breaths. "I must be brain-dead. What's the matter with me?" He looked at Amelia. "You can do it!"

"Me? What?"

"You can turn yourself into a dragon! Fly up there and look!"

"Dragon?" Jacob stepped backward and nearly sprawled down the hill.

Amelia was surprised at herself. "Why didn't I think of that?" Weird! Since they'd landed in this nowhere place, it hadn't once crossed her mind that she might take dragon shape. She got to work on it right away.

Simon watched encouragingly. Jacob knotted his fingers. Nothing happened.

Amelia tried again. She closed her eyes, held her breath, and pictured herself changing. Her head started to ache. She opened her eyes.

"Can't do it. Not here." She rubbed her forehead.

"There's got to be a way!" Simon stared up at the blotchy golden lights. "If only we had some more rocks, or a step-ladder, or…" He looked at Jacob. "But we do."

Jacob stared back, then lit up. "We have us!"

Amelia glanced down the hill. The crowd of shadow people stood looking up, but not as if they had any hope. Behind them the black flood crept nearer.

As she watched, the creeping liquid touched the heels of one of the jail guards. He wavered like a candle flame and was suddenly not there.

Amelia whirled around. "Simon!"

"I know. I saw. Come on!" He pulled at Jacob's arm. They climbed back up the pinnacle.

Amelia climbed after them. She guessed what they had in mind. A faint hope, she thought, but the only thing left to try. They stood close together on the very top. Simon made a step of his interlaced hands, and Amelia helped Jacob climb to Simon's shoulders.

Jacob teetered, swayed, balanced. Held still a long, tense moment. Reached up as if to pluck a star. Sank back.

"Can't," he said. "Too far."

"Try again." Simon braced his feet.

Amelia risked another downward look. They were stranded on a rock in the middle of a black sea. The shadow people crowded together at the base of the peak.

"It looks so close." Jacob shifted his balance on Simon's shoulders. "Just another couple of inches. I could…"

He tensed, and then leaped. He clawed upward. To Amelia it looked impossible, foolish, trying to touch the stars.

And then she saw he'd done it. He swung at arm's length, his hand hooked into a hole in the sky. He laughed aloud. Amelia laughed too, and Simon jumped and shouted. "Yes!"

Only for a moment, and then the hole ripped like paper. Jacob clung to the side of the rip. He looked through the widening gap. Golden light shone off his astonished face.

"What's happening?" Amelia hopped up and down. "Jacob!"

The rip grew. It split the dark sky open. Golden light poured in. A furious wind rushed in with it, knocking Amelia to her knees. Simon braced himself against the pinnacle. He held out an arm and she grabbed it and pulled herself in. They crouched together. The wind flooded over them, tugging ferociously.

Simon made a startled sound. Amelia raised her head. The wind had taken the shadow people. They glided overhead in a flock. They spread their arms and soared away on the gale.

Jacob suddenly sprawled at Simon's feet. "Whoa!" Simon grabbed one of his arms, Amelia the other, to keep him from flying away. And so they were firmly linked when the wind scooped them up.

They sailed in a string of three, holding hands like skydivers, under a sky leaking light from a hundred gashes. Below, the land broke into stripes of oozy darkness and glowing gold. The darkness seeped away, *like we cleared a blocked drain*, Amelia thought.

Or cleaned out a gumboil, Simon thought back at her.

This place is breaking up, came Jacob's thought.

Closing, came another thought. *Healing.*

Who was that? Amelia wondered, but nobody answered.

The distant flock of shadow-people caught the light. They shone the way flying gulls shine at sunset, high above the land. One by one, two by two, cluster by cluster, they slipped though the rifts and were gone.

Jacob, Amelia, and Simon soared together. Now there was no land, no sky, only light all around.

Jacob turned his head to smile at Simon, then at Amelia. *I really missed the sun and the stars. I'm glad—*

His hand slipped from Amelia's. *Jacob!* A speck floated in a blaze of light, and then it was gone.

Her other hand emptied. Simon was gone. Amelia screamed his name.

She whirled through the sky alone. The golden light dimmed. It turned green, then blue, then sapphire, then indigo. And then there was only the darkness.

Chapter 35

Dragon Sightings

AMELIA SPRAWLED on stone. She lay stunned and confused until something poked her in the back. When she sat up, the thing turned out to be Ike's dead flashlight.

"Is that you, Simon?" Ike quavered. "Ammy?"

"No, it's the creature from the black lagoon. Of course it's us!"

"I couldn't know. You were gone, and I was alone. In the dark. But you're back! You're okay?"

"We're okay." Simon sat up. "A bit bruised. How long were we in there?"

"I don't know. Not long. Look, I'm sorry, I just couldn't—"

Amelia looked past him. "Get back!" She pushed at both of them.

"What?" "What?"

"The door," she began, and flung up her arms to cover her face as the door cracked off its hinges. It broke into pieces as it fell. Iron chunks crashed to the ground. Bits hit their toes. Rust flakes showered through the air. Bolts and rivets bounced off the stones.

"Well, there goes the marker." Simon, unnaturally calm, picked a rivet out of his hair. "What about the gate?"

Amelia crawled forward, stood up, and crunched across the debris. She fanned a hand through the empty doorway. Then she leaned her head into it. "Not a buzz. The gate's gone."

"Closed. Healed. Like it said."

"Like who said?" Ike's voice trembled. "What happened in

207

there?"

"Tell you later," Simon said.

AMMY SAID they should leave Jacob's bones where they were until the police could come and get them. Simon thought a moment, then decided she was right.

He refused to go out by the C-shaped crevice. "It nearly cut me in half last time!"

"But we can't go up into the mall! The guards will grab us!"

"I bet not. I bet it's all over by now."

Ike and Simon were still blind as moles, so Ammy walked them, arm in arm, as far as the iron ladder. They climbed one by one, Ike first, Simon last. Pushed through the Ratman's secret entrance to the mall. Edged out from behind the plywood sheet and cat-footed through the dim lower level.

Simon watched the empty glass store fronts, and was glad to see nothing looking back at him. There were shadows here, but no ghosts or monsters.

They climbed the front escalator, which had stopped. At the top they stepped out into a crowd. Bob Lebrun stood looking down at Security One and Security Two, who sat on the floor with their heads in their hands. Kevin's father and a few of the other parents sat there too, looking dazed.

Kevin and the quints stood nearby, surrounded by the rest of the parents. Lisa Nader was talking quietly to them. Everybody except Lisa looked bewildered. Kevin had peeled off his Peer Monitor nametag and was looking at it as if he was wondering how it had gotten on his shirt.

"Keep your face turned away," Ammy murmured. She walked, not fast and not slow, around the outside of the crowd towards the place where the front doors should have been. Night air blew in through a big gap. Broken glass crunched under their shoes.

Oscar was writing in his notebook and listening to one of the mothers. Simon caught some of it as he sidled past. "It was terrible," she was saying. "It was just so crazy. The guards and the boys barricaded themselves on the mezzanine. They threw stink bombs — they'd made them up in the apothecary shop. People could have really got hurt! And then, about ten minutes ago, just like that! It all fizzled out. Just stopped. I've never seen anything like it."

They almost made it. Another dozen steps and they would have been home free. Then Lisa Nader spotted them. She pointed. "You three! Again!"

It took them twenty minutes to get out of that one. They did a good job of telling the truth without mentioning Mythrin, dragons, or cosmic gates, Simon thought.

"The Rat— I mean, Mr. Ralston," Ammy finished. "He can back us up. He was down there too. He told us all about Buckingham Palace, and how Jacob got there."

Lisa looked around. "Has anybody seen Harry Ralston?" Nobody had.

CELESTE CAME marching in just then and led Ammy and Simon away by their elbows. Ammy's parents drove up from Toronto and stayed overnight. The older generations sat in the kitchen talking into the small hours. Ammy went home the next day.

Simon went to school on Tuesday morning wearing the sandals Ty had wrecked, mended with heavy-duty staples and duct tape. The talk was all about Kevin Purcell and yesterday's amazing events in the mall. Kevin was strangely quiet. So were the quints, who were carefully staying away from each other.

A rumour started up that Simon Hammer had discovered some caves under the mall, with a body in one of them, like in that film,

The Mummy. The rumour died out by lunchtime because nothing so exciting would ever happen to Simon, obviously.

The stories about the gigantic flying lizard were something else again. This was real news. Ike went into the school library in the morning and found articles on the Internet. He printed copies and shared them with everybody in the lunchroom at noon.

There were three confirmed sightings, all on Monday evening. One by some people in the CN Tower, one by the pilot of a small airplane near Kitchener, and one by three German tourists who were on the Dunning Street bridge when the creature rose from the gorge.

Vern Sparks claimed he'd seen the same creature on Saturday night, when it had tried to carry off his Volkswagen. There were claw marks on the car's roof to prove it. The photo he'd taken with his cell phone had been published in the *Toronto Sun*, but it was so smudgy that you couldn't tell what the flying thing was, just that it was big.

Ike ran an opinion poll on the web: WHAT WAS IT? He got a couple of hundred hits and posted the results Tuesday night. The top five opinions were that the creature was: (1) a bald eagle, (2) a turkey vulture, (3) fog, (4) a hoax, and (5) something to do with global warming.

Ike told Simon about his other news after school. The bones in the cave had been taken away. "And my dad says they're going to follow up on our tip. They'll try and find out if Jacob Redding has any relatives living. They'll do DNA testing. Maybe Jacob will end up being buried with his family after all."

"I hope he does," Simon said. "He missed them."

They went to Bruce's Coffee and Doughnut. It was crowded: the mall was closed for renovation again. "They're getting rid of those old stones," Bruce said. "Good thing, too."

"I bet Harry Ralston won't like that," Ike said.

"Well, Harry's not here to say, is he?"

They captured a corner booth. Ike was all eyebrows. "Harry's still missing?"

"Remember I told you we saw him in that shadow place? I think he must've let the gate eat him up, bit by bit, over the years. He was a sort of shadow himself. I don't think he'll be back."

"Whoa." Ike sat back and stuffed his mouth with jelly doughnut.

Simon waited for the next question. He knew it was bound to come.

"So, who put up the starry window?"

"I think it was the gate itself."

"The gate," Ike said, muffled through the doughnut.

"Not just that gate. All of them everywhere. Together. I think the system of gates is alive. Like a brain and nervous system. Like a person."

Ike dropped his doughnut and showered the table with icing sugar.

"And I think what happened to that gate under the mall was a kind of cancer."

Ike chewed and pondered and swallowed. "You helped cut out the bad part, before the cancer could spread."

Simon picked up his walnut cruller. "That's right," he said with satisfaction. "We saved the gates."

SIMON WOKE suddenly. His clock said it was half past two in the morning. He was sinking back to sleep when a noise at the window pulled him upright.

Someone was hanging outside his window, looking in.

The figure was holding onto the outside of the window frame with fingers and toes. It freed one hand to gesture upward.

Simon peered at it. "Okay." He got up, put on his dressing gown and slippers, and quietly let himself out of the apartment.

When he climbed out onto the roof, a tall, dark-faced man was waiting for him. The moon reflected pale purple from his eyes.

"Tarq."

"No more. I am John Lilac."

"But why?"

Lilac spread his extra-jointed fingers in a wide shrug. "I am a creature under enchantment. Perhaps I read too many books, learned too much of human thought. I know only that there is one place for me, and that is here. With Vesper."

"But what about your people?"

"My friend, the one you call Pirrip, will lead them until they can choose a new chief. They will do well."

"Does Mara know?"

"My sister?" Lilac lifted his long nose, and for a moment looked scarily dragon-like. "My sister has no say in this. But it's good you remind me. I have a thing to do for her. Show me what is in your pocket."

"What?" Simon's hand slid into his dressing gown pocket and closed.

"The stone in your pocket." Lilac scooped a hand impatiently. "Show it!"

Simon brought it out and uncurled his fingers. "I suppose she wants it back."

"Not the stone, no." Lilac narrowed his eyes at it, then picked it up. He tossed it from hand to hand. In the dark it grew a halo of blue flame, which quickly faded. He tossed it back to Simon, who dropped it, thinking it would be hot. But when he picked it up, it was barely warm.

There was a difference, though. Simon held it up to the moonlight and turned it over and over. He looked at John Lilac.

"Yes, that is gone." Lilac's mouth bent: almost a smile. "Did you

212

think she would not know the smell of dragon's blood? Especially her own?"

"It was Mara's blood? I didn't know!"

"No matter. What you have now is just a stone."

"It's a stone from Mythrin. That's not just a stone."

"Keep it well, then. For me, that door is closed." John Lilac turned away without another word, slipped over the parapet, and was gone.

Chapter 36
Godzilla

"NO," AMMY SAID to Simon on the phone on Tuesday evening, "they never did ask how I got to Dunstone, and so fast. I think they were afraid to find out I hitched with some speed-demon biker. They kept on at me most of the way home about the dangers of hitchhiking. Like I'd be so dumb!"

"So, no school today?"

"Not exactly. We all went to school today, the three of us, and talked to my teachers. And guess what's weird? Mr. DeSouza thinks there's good stuff in me. At least that's what he said."

"That's g—"

"But you want to hear the best? My dad asked me what I really want to do. I said, fly. So, get this. They've promised me flying lessons if I get an A average by the end of grade nine."

"An A average? Wow! Think you can do it?"

"Of course I can. If I try. I'm just not sure it's worth it."

"But if you really want to fly...."

"It'll be cool. Just, not as good as the real thing."

"HEY THERE, Godzilla."

Amelia froze, bent over, with her hands in her backpack. *So now it starts.* She finished zipping her backpack and straightened up without any hurry.

Petra stood staring down at her, using all her extra inches. It was

214

the end of classes on Wednesday. Other kids jostled past.

"Say that again?" Amelia imagined her eyes dragon-gold, cat-slit. She half-lidded them dangerously.

Petra narrowed hers. "Suppose I call you Barney instead. Better?"

Amelia's hands curled. She imagined claws. She opened her mouth.

Then a thought struck her. She'd been at school all day and nobody had given her the evil eye. In fact, some kids had spoken to her as if she were normal. Like that boy Dougie Tam. It was like none of them knew what a monster walked among them.

She uncurled her hands. "Barney is a dinosaur. A *stuffed* dinosaur."

Petra bit down on her lip.

"You didn't tell anybody, did you?"

"Who would believe me? Man, you're so easy to needle."

They walked together out of the school and around the corner to Queen Street.

"So, what are you?" Petra asked casually.

"Part dragon, I think. I wasn't born that way. It's just since last winter. And I'm not very good at it, yet."

They walked on another half block in easy silence. It was warm for late October. Something heavy lifted from Amelia's chest a little more with each step they took together.

"Okay," Petra said at last. "I saw it. I have to believe my own eyes." She hitched her backpack higher. "That story in the news yesterday? About the CN Tower?"

"Yeah, that was me."

"Wicked! Don't suppose you could teach me how to do that. Become a dragon."

"I'm pretty sure not. Sorry. It happened to me by accident. I think

215

you have to share a dragon's dreams. And I think maybe you have to go to Mythrin, too."

"Mythrin? Where's Mythrin? *What's* Mythrin?"

Amelia stopped at the corner of Queen Street and Chrysoprase Road. She looked south, towards the lake. From here it was one long block downhill to the boardwalk and the beach and the shining blue water. You could hear the gulls crying over the growl of traffic.

Something else down there, too. Amelia squinted, sharpened her focus. Then laughed aloud. "How much time have you got?"

"As long as you like. Why?"

"C'mon."

She steered Petra across the intersection southward, then down the hill towards the beach. At the edge of the water, a tall girl in a glittery red jacket was skipping stones.

Chapter 37

Jacob Goes Home

THE DUNSTONE INDEPENDENT
One Mystery Solved, Two Still Murky
by Oscar Vogelsang, Editor-in-Chief
Dunstone, December 20

More than 70 years after he went missing, Jacob Redding has been reunited with his family, thanks to local teens.

Newspapers across the country headlined the discovery on October 23 of the skeletal remains of a young boy in previously unknown caves beneath the Dunstone Mall.

The find was made by two Dunstone teens, Simon Hammer and Isaac Vogelsang, with the help of Simon's cousin, Amelia Hammer, of Toronto.

A combination of historical research and DNA testing at the Ontario Centre of Forensic Sciences confirmed that the remains were those of Jacob Redding, a 14-year-old inmate of the Dunstone Training School who probably died about the time the school was closed, in 1931.

The cause of death is still uncertain.

Since a full sister of Jacob's is still living —

Mrs. Alice Kendall of Toronto, born 1937 — it was possible to positively identify the remains through DNA testing.

"It's such a sad story, but at least now it's over," Mrs. Kendall says. "I know my parents never stopped grieving. Now he will rest in peace next to them. I can't thank those three kids enough."

The three teens were present at a memorial service held for Jacob on Saturday in St. Thomas's Anglican Church, Toronto. Interment took place in Mount Pleasant Cemetery.

Although one local mystery is solved, two others remain on the books. Harry Ralston, manager of the Dunstone Mall, has been missing since the day Jacob Redding's remains were discovered.

"It's like he just fell down a black hole," said one employee, who refused to be identified. Police are investigating.

Coincidentally, the young man identified as Ty Jones, who first attracted police attention as a streaker at the Dunstone Mall on October 20, and shortly afterward survived a fall into the Dunn River gorge, has also not been seen since October 23.

In the case of Jones, there is no reason to suspect foul play, according to OPP Constable Lisa Nader. It is believed he has left the district.

About the author

PATRICIA BOW lives in Kitchener, Ontario. She has written six other books for young people. To find out more about Patricia and her work, visit www.execulink.com/~thebows/patricia.htm.